YAKUP ALMELEK

THE GOVERNESS

İstanbul–Zürich–London

YAKUP ALMELEK

THE GOVERNESS

Translated from the Turkish
by Alvin Parmar

PUBLISHING

Library of Congress Control Number: 2008932190

AP 004

www.arionpublishing.co.uk

arion@arionpublishing.co.uk

First Published in English, August 2008 – Arion Publishing
30 Amberwood Parkway, Ashland, OH 44805, USA

© ARION Yayınevi, İstanbul
Dadı, 2008

All rights reserved. No part of this book may be reprinted or reproduced or utilised in any form or by any electronic, mechanical, or other means, now known or hereafter invented, including photocopying and recording, or in any information storage or retrieval system, without permission in writing from the Publishers.

Address: PK 395 34433 Sirkeci / İSTANBUL-TR

Printed in Turkey by Barış Printing.
Davutpaşa Cad. Güven Sanayi Sitesi C Blok No: 219 Topkapı / İstanbul
Tel: +90 212 674 85 28

ISBN 978-9944-0709-8-0

I was in London one weekend. I had left the book I had wanted to take with me at home. I went down to the hotel kiosk. I counted the books: there were exactly ten and I had not heard of any of the authors before. I asked the young man working there to give me a book that was easy to read, but at the same time interesting.

He sized up each book carefully and decided on one of them. "OK, I've found what you're looking for. Here you are." I looked at the book he reached out to me. It was written by someone called "Roald Dahl"… The young man explained who he was.

I thanked him for his trouble and went back up to my room. I curled up in an armchair and dived into the book that I had just bought. About two hours later, I went back to the kiosk. The young man there asked as soon as he saw me: "So, did you like it then?" I answered without even having to think about it: "It's a great book. The stories are wonderful!"

He was very happy that I had liked the book he had recommended. It was clear from the look on his face.

I asked him for a notebook with squared paper, a pencil, an eraser and a pencil sharpener. He asked me rather hesitantly if I was going to be writing a letter. I told him that I was going to write a play. I was inspired!

Having bought all the equipment necessary to write a play from the young man, I went back up to my room, sat down at the desk and set about putting *The Governess* down onto paper.

Each line that I wrote brought me great pleasure. If you have a similar pleasure reading or watching *The Governess*, I shall be one of the happiest people in the world.

Yakup Almelek
İstanbul, 28th April 2008

About the author:

Yakup Almelek was born in Ankara in 1936 and attended Ankara College. After finishing high school there, he moved to Istanbul with his family in 1955. He graduated from the School of Economics and Commerce in İstanbul.

Starting from fifth grade, he would work during every summer holiday. Among other things, he worked as an accountant's assistant and tried his hand at marketing. He learnt much from the experience that all these summer jobs gave him, and many of the incidents he lived through then, incidents which reflect human nature and Turkey in those days, appear in his articles and short stories.

In 1967, he founded his own company, now in its forty-first year.

Ever since middle school, alongside his professional life, he has indulged his inner life: *reading and writing*... He has written poetry, verse, marches, stories, newspaper articles and plays. While he was still at school, one of his articles won a competition and was published in *Cumhuriyet* newspaper. In the years that followed, more of his writing appeared in the newspaper. He now writes a regular column for *Şalom*.

One of his short stories has been turned into a film and three of his plays – *The Businessman, The Awakening* and *The Governess* – have been staged.

Yakup Almelek is married with two children.

Characters

Ahmet Beyaz, a businessman in his sixties.

Leyla Beyaz, Ahmet Beyaz' wife. In her fifties, a housewife.

Songül Beyaz, their daughter, thirty years old.

The Judge, a retired appeals-court judge, in his sixties.

The Judge's Wife, in her fifties, a housewife.

The Governess, the woman who has brought Songül up since her birth, in her sixties.

The Wine Doctor, Orhan Gün, referred to as the Wine Doctor throughout the play.

Act One

The sitting room. It immediately catches the eye that the room is furnished in a rather showy way. It is clear that the people who live here like to spend money. The appearance of the house is a projection of their way of life.

There are paintings on the wall, a carpet on the floor, a statue, the table in the middle is laid for seven; on the left, there are armchairs; there is a bookcase on the wall.

The curtain rises to the sound of cheerful music.

In one of the armchairs, Ahmet Beyaz is sitting. He is dapper and looks slightly agitated. As he flicks randomly through the pages of a magazine, it is clear that his mind is on other things.

In the armchair opposite him, his wife, Leyla Beyaz is sitting with her legs crossed reading a book. She is calm and looks at her husband lovingly; they smile at each other.

Their daughter, Songül, enters. She is wearing jeans and a t-shirt. She is sulking about something and greets her mother and father moodily.

SONGÜL: Hello.

AHMET BEYAZ: Hello, why the long face? To look at you, anyone'd think you'd lost a fiver and found a penny.

SONGÜL: (*Angry and on the verge of tears*) No, dad, I haven't lost a fiver; I've lost a whole plane.

AHMET BEYAZ: Now what's that supposed to mean? I don't get it.

SONGÜL: Dad, you know full well what I'm talking about

THE GOVERNESS

'cause it was you who made the call.

AHMET BEYAZ: And where am I supposed to have called?

SONGÜL: There's an amateur flying club; they teach you how to fly one-man and two-man planes. It would have been such a good laugh. I put my name down, and you, you called and had them remove it, and, as if that wasn't enough, you gave them a telling off and yelled down the phone at them, too!

AHMET BEYAZ: Well, they made such a song and dance of everything! But why would I have given them a telling off or yelled at them?

SONGÜL: The club's accountant told you it was me who put my name down and if I'd changed my mind, it should be me who goes and tells them. And when he said that, oh, you really blew your top! "I'm Ahmet Beyaz," you yelled at them, "and if you don't take my daughter's name off your list, I'll make you wish you'd never been born!" Now, dad, that was hardly a respectable way to go about now, was it?

AHMET BEYAZ: Well, I suppose not... (*Looking at his wife*) Leyla, say something, will you?

LEYLA BEYAZ: (*Raising her head from her book, it is clear that she has been listening to them carefully, but pretending to read*) But you went and put your name down without telling us, dear, now that's not anything to be proud of either.

SONGÜL: Ah, mum! I'm thirty years old! Why do you keep treating me like a child?

LEYLA BEYAZ:	Now come on, darling, let's not make mountains out of mole-hills! We don't treat you like a child; you're all grown-up now! No one's keeping you locked up, now, are they?
SONGÜL:	This living and breathing soul is my soul. Aren't we all gifts from God? So, let me use my gift however I want!
LEYLA BEYAZ:	Darling, we weren't thinking with our heads; we were thinking with our hearts. We let our hearts rule our heads. When it comes to you, it's not logic that's in charge, it's feelings.
AHMET BEYAZ:	Where did you come up with the idea of being a pilot, anyway, darling? We were worried; it's so dangerous.
SONGÜL:	Driving is even more dangerous! Just take a look at all the car accidents! You can be sure that planes are safer.
AHMET BEYAZ:	But, darling, you can't just make your decisions like that! Do the pilots there know how to teach? What kind of planes do they use? You have to look into all of that; then we'll see.
SONGÜL:	For God's sake, dad, why don't you let me live a little? Now tell me the truth, dad, did the governess snitch on me, telling you I'd signed up for flying lessons?
AHMET BEYAZ:	What? You mean she knew, but you hid it from us?
SONGÜL:	No, I swear, I didn't tell her.

AHMET BEYAZ:	So, how come she'd know, then?
SONGÜL:	I've got a friend in the club, and her mum got to know the governess at school; she must have said something.
AHMET BEYAZ:	In this house, I'm always the last to know anything. It's not me who's the head of this family; it's the governess!
SONGÜL:	Come on, dad, it's not that bad! I didn't tell anyone I'd put my name down for flying lessons; honestly, I didn't even tell the governess. Anyway, where did you find out about it?
AHMET BEYAZ:	A relative of one of your friends in the flying school works in our factory. He told me that you'd signed up. Has the governess ever told me anything? She'd sooner die than give up a secret.
SONGÜL:	Alright, alright, they've taken my name off the list anyway. We've got nothing left to fight about.
AHMET BEYAZ:	And that's exactly how it should be.
SONGÜL:	Look, I really do love you; I love the governess, too, of course, but you should give me more freedom. For example, I want to have a flat of my own, you know, one of those studio things.
AHMET BEYAZ:	(*Mockingly and angrily*) Whatever for? Aren't you comfortable here?
SONGÜL:	Dad, you know I think it's great living with you. But it's a fact that young people need to have their

freedom. Think about Europe or America. You leave home there when you're eighteen.

AHMET BEYAZ: But they're not the same as us.

SONGÜL: When it suits you, you say we should be more like them, and when it doesn't, you say they're not the same as us!

LEYLA BEYAZ: (*Raising her head from the book she was pretending to read*) Stop this bickering! Songül, go and get changed, our guests will be here soon.

SONGÜL: What's wrong with what I'm wearing?

LEYLA BEYAZ: Well, you can hardly meet guests dressed like that, now can you?

SONGÜL: (*Turning to her father*) Dad, if you only knew just how expensive these jeans and t-shirt are, which mum has taken such exception to! Me and guvvie spent a small fortune on them!

AHMET BEYAZ: It doesn't matter.

SONGÜL: You shouldn't spoil me so much.

LEYLA BEYAZ: I know, it's your father who spoils you, not me.

SONGÜL: I could find a job and earn some money; that way I'd know the value of what I'm spending. But dad won't let me. Mum, you're right, dad spoils me.

AHMET BEYAZ: Well, you both put it so well! It's all my fault! We'll talk about this another day, OK? I'm not really on

	form at the moment...
SONGÜL:	OK, dad, so who's coming to tea? I didn't know we were expecting guests.
AHMET BEYAZ:	You hear us talking about them all the time, darling. Metin Çelik, the retired judge. He used to sit on the appeals court. His wife's coming, too, and there's that Orhan, you know, the one they call "le docteur du vin".
SONGÜL:	Who? Oh, it's OK, I remember now. The judge and his wife and Orhan, the wineseller.
AHMET BEYAZ:	He's not a wineseller; he's a wine doctor, le docteur du vin!
SONGÜL:	It was a slip of the tongue. Anyway, I suppose the judge and his wife are important. His wife's a bit pasty-faced, but anyway. But this Orhan, I mean, isn't he a wineseller? He imports and exports wine: that's selling. And where did he get his doctorate from? For all we know, he probably gave himself the title. Is there even such a thing as a "docteur du vin"?
AHMET BEYAZ:	You and the governess haven't got a good word to say about anyone. The French gave him that title, so there must be something like that in France.
SONGÜL:	God, dad, you must have been born yesterday! Sometimes it's so difficult to understand you. You're an intelligent businessman, yet you fall for this fake doctor stuff. I sometimes wonder about you!

AHMET BEYAZ: It's in all the French papers. I've read them. It's true.

SONGÜL: Which French papers? I'm guessing we're not talking about *Le Figaro* here. No, don't tell me, *Paris Match* gave our wineseller a doctorate. You know, like we saw on TV a few years back: Sementa, the woman who could move her nose left, right, forwards and backwards. And all of a sudden the wineseller's a wine doctor.

AHMET BEYAZ: It's all in the governess' head. She never took to him in the first place. She never likes anyone anyway. What did she say about Orhan?

SONGÜL: She said he was "faul".

AHMET BEYAZ: And what's that supposed to mean?

SONGÜL: Good-for-nothing, living of others, inept... according to her and my understanding of the term, anyway.

LEYLA BEYAZ: (*Raising her head from her book, to her husband*) Let her go and get changed, Ahmet. The guests are practically here.

AHMET BEYAZ: For God's sake, is it me stopping her from getting changed? Who do you think keeps arguing with everything I say?

SONGÜL: Don't worry, mum, my stuff's all ready. I'll be all made up and beautiful in a flash! Anyway, hasn't the boy in that novel you're reading kissed the girl yet?

LEYLA BEYAZ: (*Pointing at the book in amazement*) Have you read it?

SONGÜL: No, of course not, but there's always a happy ending in that kind of book. Husband and wife get back together, daughter-in-law gives mother-in-law a hug, and the boy kisses the girl; everyone's dreams come true, and we can all sleep easily.

LEYLA BEYAZ: I hope that's how your life turns out.

SONGÜL: God, mum, I've got better things to think about than that.

LEYLA BEYAZ: You shouldn't forget these things though; they should be at the top of your list.

SONGÜL: (*Turning to her father*) Dad, could you please tell mum not to open this topic again; I don't like it at all.

AHMET BEYAZ: Well, I don't know about that; I'll think about it while you're getting changed!

SONGÜL: You'd think I was standing here naked from what you're saying! My clothes are very stylish, actually, and I've got the price tags to prove it. Nowadays, yuppies are always going into management meetings wearing clothes like mine.

LEYLA BEYAZ: (*Raising her head from her book*) Who? Who did you say?

SONGÜL: Mum, are you listening to us or are you reading your book?

LEYLA BEYAZ: Both of them, darling. But what did you just say? Who's wearing clothes like yours?

SONGÜL: Yuppies.

LEYLA BEYAZ: I've never heard of them. Who are the yuppies? And what do they wear, whoever they are?

SONGÜL: Who are the yuppies? Young, urban professionals, mum, they're peace-loving, intelligent and green. What do they wear? Jeans, white, long-sleeved shirts, gold cufflinks and designer ties. If you want to be a Yuppie, you've definitely got to have gone to a foreign university. And of course, for all of that, you need a pretty well-off dad.

LEYLA BEYAZ: OK, then, so those are men. Are there girl yuppies, too? You could be called a Yuppie, too, couldn't you?

SONGÜL: There are girl Yuppies, but I'm not one of them, and you want to know why? 'Cause I didn't study abroad.

LEYLA BEYAZ: Don't you worry, you'll see, one day, your dad will send you to London... with your governess, of course.

AHMET BEYAZ: OK, that's enough! Now go and get changed, darling.

SONGÜL: (*Turning to her mother*) You see what tactics he's using to change the subject, don't you, mum? Anyway, I'll get my gladrags on and tart myself up like an old filmstar. (*She exits dancing. She enters again a few seconds later and walks towards the audience. The lights go down, Ahmet and Leyla Beyaz remain in the background.)*

SONGÜL: Ladies and gentlemen, you heard what mum said a little earlier, "No one's keeping you locked up, now, are they?" By biggest dream is to have a place of my own, but whenever I bring up the subject, dad always says, "Aren't you happy here?" I'd love to get a job and earn some money, but no, with dad it's always, "We've got two factories; what's the point in going to someone else's door, cap in hand?"

I'm thirty years old. I should be financially independent. I should be getting a small flat with the money I earn and living how I want.

But we just can't agree! Dad says him and mum should be an example to me.

We're living today, and today means now. Today means preparing for tomorrow; it means the future. I want to live today; I don't want to go back to yesterday.

And so, my elders and betters, here's what I think: we are new, try to understand us. Don't go expecting us to understand you, though. We can't turn the clock back.

It wouldn't be right for me to complain about my mum and dad and about the governess to you. I love them all dearly. Without them, the world would have no joy, but still they've got to start respecting my own personal preferences, too.

I'll just say one more thing and then I'm off.

They're really keen on marrying me off. The other day, dad, half-joking and half-deadly serious, muttered, "Are there no eligible men left, then?" Now, I'm not against having a family; it's a social and sexual necessity, but there are limits.

Dad seems to think this bloke they call the wine doctor would be good for me. He looks decent and has an air of politeness and culture. He was educated in France and knows a few languages. Ooh, we could open a translation agency together! I mean, that's all well and good, but it doesn't exactly get the fires of passion burning.

And it's not like I don't already have a boyfriend. The governess doesn't even know very much about him yet.

Before doing anything, I'll see what she has to say, then I'll ask mum. The governess keeps saying she's my real mother too. Not that she gave birth to me, but I'm supposed to be the little girl she lost in an accident. Reincarnation, transmigration of souls, metempsychosis, abracadabra... and the soul of her dead daughter passed into my body at the moment of my birth. But you'll hear about that later.

Anyway, enjoy the rest of the show. See you later. (*Exits.*)

(*The lights come back on; Leyla and Ahmet Beyaz remain on stage.*)

LEYLA BEYAZ: Well, thank God we got over the plane incident. I was worried she was going to fly off the handle and start crying.

AHMET BEYAZ: The governess must have given her a talking to. I mean, do you really think she'd have caved in so easily otherwise? But listen, you keep giving her ideas about England this, England that. Hasn't she got enough education? She is a graduate, after all, so what's all this about studying abroad? You'd be better off looking for a husband for her.

LEYLA BEYAZ: But darling, times have changed: girls find their own husbands nowadays.

AHMET BEYAZ: But she doesn't like anyone! What's she looking for? A knight in shining armour to come riding in on his white horse?

LEYLA BEYAZ: There's a French saying: "Every young woman looks for the man of her dreams, but while she's waiting, she doesn't forget to get married."

AHMET BEYAZ: I'm not the one you should be telling. Try telling that to Songül. But wait a minute, you mean I wasn't the man of your dreams? I'm just the man you got married to while you were waiting for him to turn up?

LEYLA BEYAZ: Of course not! I really liked you, as soon as I laid eyes on you. You were different.

AHMET BEYAZ: In what way?

LEYLA BEYAZ: The man of my dreams was more handsome, but, I mean, that's normal; we always exaggerate in our dreams... But you were more successful than the man of my dreams, more intelligent. Anyway, what about you?

AHMET BEYAZ: Of course, I had my dreams, what man doesn't? But as soon as I saw you, I said to myself, now there's the girl I'm going to spend the rest of my life with. Exactly those words!

(*The Governess, The Judge and The Judge's Wife enter. Ahmet and Leyla Beyaz rise to their feet as soon as they see them.*)

LEYLA-AHMET BEYAZ: Oh, do come in! How are you? (*They embrace each other.*) We're so glad you were able to come.

AHMET BEYAZ: (*To The Judge*) Well, anyway, how are things, your honour?

THE JUDGE: Well, what can I say? I lead a life of solitude. Ever since I retired, we've been very isolated from the rest of the world; everyone who used to call by on us, they've all disappeared. But we support each other as husband and wife. We're lucky we've got each other.

AHMET BEYAZ: Now, you became a judge, and you sat on the court of appeal, why did you always steer clear of politics? I mean, you're retired now, why don't you join some party that appeals to you?

THE JUDGE: To go into politics you need to have the right mental and intellectual make-up. If you don't, there's no point, they'll throw you to the lions and there'll be no one there to pick up the pieces.

LEYLA BEYAZ: But this country needs honest, honourable men like you. If no one wants to get their hands dirty with politics, what's going to happen to the country?

THE JUDGE: Thanks for the vote of confidence. But you know, our society isn't really in need of honest people. If it was, they'd have been in charge long ago. But we don't like the politicians we've got, well, whose fault is that? No one's. Or rather, it's not even a question of fault. We're all pretty much the same, when it comes down to it, and today we have people who are pretty much the same as us in government. And these people who are pretty much the same as us rule us in a way we can understand. It's that simple.

THE GOVERNESS: But the Italians made reforms; they brought transparency to politics. Can't we do the same here?

THE JUDGE: We're not the same as the Italians: they have a stronger economy, and as for culture, well, it's one of the top countries in Europe. Once a society gets to a certain standard of living, it doesn't just want the quantity, it wants the quality too. It objects to any abuses that are too obvious and tries to give the impression it's doing something about it. That's what the Italians did.

THE GOVERNESS: Well, why don't we do the same? Why don't we put our intellectuals in power and have everyone support them?

THE JUDGE: Most people are happy with their lot, and as for fine words, well, there's always plenty of them! Who doesn't like hot air? If anyone says they're honest, they should come and prove it. Everyone always wants everyone else to be honest, as long as it doesn't affect them.

LEYLA BEYAZ:	For example?
THE JUDGE:	There are many examples. People from all walks of life. Businessmen, bureaucrats, civil servants, tradesmen, the self-employed, farmers, villagers... in short, everyone, civilians, soldiers, everyone should be transparent in the social sphere. We always talk about having clean hands and about transparent government. What does that mean? It means paying your taxes honestly, it means not taking bribes, it means declaring your income truthfully. If you haven't got these, you haven't got anything.
THE GOVERNESS:	I read in the paper the other day that we need open government.
THE JUDGE:	Yes, I was coming to that. Transparency is the only solution. With us, everyone wants everyone else's hands to be spotless, but their own hands, well that's a different thing altogether... first them, then me, that's what we always say. But that's not how it works. If you want clean hands, first wash your own, then look at everyone else's hands.
THE GOVERNESS:	Sometimes I'm so pessimistic. I mean, who's going to get everything back on the straight and narrow?
THE JUDGE:	Don't be pessimistic; I've pinned my hopes on the youth of today and the future generation. They think differently to us. We can't keep holding on to our principles in the face of civilisation. There's only one way forward.
LEYLA BEYAZ:	Yes, when lots of European countries are heading

THE GOVERNESS

> towards honesty and transparency, we seem to be going in the opposite direction!

THE JUDGE: Listen, why don't we leave saving the country for another day? I'm looking at the table and see it's set for seven, now, with Songül, that makes six, so who's the lucky seventh?

THE JUDGE'S WIFE: Yes, where is Songül? We'd really like to see her.

AHMET BEYAZ: She's gone to get changed, she'll be down any moment now. The other guest is Orhan Gün, otherwise known as "the wine doctor".

THE GOVERNESS: (*To The Judge and The Judge's Wife*) If you'd excuse me just a moment, I'll be back soon.

THE JUDGE: Of course. (*The Governess exits.*) A wine doctor, eh? I didn't know there was such a branch of medicine. What exactly is a wine doctor?

AHMET BEYAZ: We met a couple of months ago; he's from Istanbul. He has a sad story. He lost his parents when he was little, I think when he was still in primary school. He was sent to live with a relative in Marseilles. He studied and worked there at the same time. Anyway, it's a wine-growing, or should I say grape-growing, region. And I guess he was just talented from birth. When he tastes a wine, he can tell straight away which one it is.

THE JUDGE'S WIFE: Yes, I read somewhere about people like that, they're like computers. They drink a little of any wine, and their brain – just like a computer – records the year and the region. If they taste the

	same wine again, even if it's many years later, their brain makes the association and they can tell you what it is immediately.
THE JUDGE:	Wait, wait, I think I remember now; it was in the papers, wasn't it? Someone inherited a mansion on the Bosphorus, or something ...
LEYLA BEYAZ:	Yes, and on the most exclusive part of the Bosphorus, too.
AHMET BEYAZ:	So, anyway, he came back from Marseilles because a distant relative died in a car accident here, and he was the sole heir. And he ended up with that mansion that all the papers are talking about, a mansion worth God only knows how many million dollars.
THE JUDGE:	Well, what does he do now?
AHMET BEYAZ:	He's opened a little office for himself. He's importing and exporting wine. But, I mean, he's only been back in Turkey a couple of months.
THE JUDGE:	So, you're saying he tastes the wine and then tells you it's year and region?
AHMET BEYAZ:	Yes, my friend, that's exactly it. First, he sniffs it, then he tastes it and he tells you the year and the region.
THE JUDGE:	Well, have you ever seen him do it? Or is it just something they use to fill up the newspapers?
AHMET BEYAZ:	Oh, we've seen it, right here, in this very room.

THE GOVERNESS

THE JUDGE: Oh, tell me more! I'm dying to know more about it.

AHMET BEYAZ: Well, I can see why you were a judge! You want witnesses for everything! The word "hair-splitting" could have been invented for you! Well, are you sitting comfortably? Then I'll begin. We're going back in time thirty days.

(*The lights go down. The Wine Doctor, Ahmet Beyaz, Leyla Beyaz, Songül and The Governess are around the table. The Judge and The Judge's Wife are behind, watching.*)

AHMET BEYAZ: (*To The Wine Doctor*) Now, my friend, seeing the best French newspapers call you "the wine doctor", can I call you that, too?

THE WINE DOCTOR: Of course, I'd be honoured.

AHMET BEYAZ: Now, don't misunderstand me, but if we give you a glass of wine, could you tell us where it's from and which year it is? Of course, we're not trying to test you; I mean, I wouldn't want you to think we didn't believe you.

THE WINE DOCTOR: Oh, I would never think that! I know what I can do, I've given so much of my life to wine, and they saw fit to award me with the title of doctor. Why should I feel put out at that? After all, you've got to put your money where your mouth is. So, go ahead, I'm at your service.

AHMET BEYAZ: At our service? You flatter us! (*Turning to Songül*) Darling, can you bring one of the bottles from the shelf in the study? And don't forget to take the label off.

SONGÜL: (*Reluctantly*) Alright, dad, I'll bring one. (*She exits*) (*Songül enters with a bottle of wine in her hand.*)

AHMET BEYAZ: Now, why don't you open it and pour out a glass, darling.

SONGÜL: A wine glass, or will a normal water glass do?

AHMET BEYAZ: (*Trying to hide his annoyance*) What difference does it make? He's only going to take a sip of the stuff, aren't you?

SONGÜL: I wouldn't want to seem disrespectful in front of the doctor.

THE WINE DOCTOR: Please, just a glass, it's not important what kind, any kind will do. You did remember to take the label off, didn't you, Miss Beyaz?

SONGÜL: I did, sir, and I put it in my pocket. Now I'm pouring the wine into a normal water glass. (*She pours out a glass of wine*)

AHMET BEYAZ: What do you say to a little wager on your wine-tasting abilities, you know, just to make the occasion a little more fun? If you win, I'll give you something, and if you lose, you'll give me something.

THE WINE DOCTOR: Yes, why not? What did you have in mind?

AHMET BEYAZ: (*Turning to his wife*) Leyla, why don't you choose the stake?

LEYLA BEYAZ:	Well, what about a tie? You'd remember this evening every time you wore it.
THE WINE DOCTOR:	Yes, a tie's a good idea.
AHMET BEYAZ:	And it's fine with me, too.
THE WINE DOCTOR:	Well, I shall now take a sip of wine from this glass. In a few minutes, I hope to be able to tell you it's region and year. Of course, I could be mistaken. We are all human, and to err is human, after all. But, I don't want to embarrass myself in front of friends such as you. So I'll be trying my very best to pass this test. If I get it wrong, please don't think any less of me. (*He raises the glass to his lips and lowers it again without drinking.*) One more thing. Let me remind you that I need complete silence. Once the wine has touched my lips, I will search for its region and year. Please do not tap your feet or do anything with your hands, do not take deep breaths. I shall be entering a transcendental meditative state, and even the rustle of a leaf could be enough to prevent me finding the right answer. (*He takes a sip*)

The wine is caressing my lips. I am becoming one with it. I am making love with it. (*As he is speaking, Ahmet Beyaz, Leyla Beyaz and Songül wait motionlessly, as if they are holding their breath. However, there is a faint smile on The Governess' lips.*)

(*30 seconds later*)

But you gave me something easy! I've been trained for much more difficult wines. It's a 1986 Tekirdağ.

AHMET BEYAZ: Yes! You got it, didn't he, Songül? Check the label, dear...

SONGÜL: (*Looking at the label she has taken out of her pocket*) Yes, dad, he got it. The region and the year are both correct...

AHMET BEYAZ: Well, my friend, they were right to call you the Wine Doctor; well done, bravo.

LEYLA BEYAZ: Yes, well done Orhan, sorry, Doctor. How did you do it?

SONGÜL: Bravo Orhan, sorry, Doctor!

(*The Governess smiles at them with a slightly angry look in her eye and exits without congratulating The Wine Doctor.*)

AHMET BEYAZ: Well, my dear doctor, I say we drink to your success! Songül, dear, could you pour the wine out into the real wine glasses this time, please. Let us drink a toast to the Doctor! But where's the governess? Didn't she congratulate the doctor? Well, she believes in all sorts of strange things, doctor, don't take it personally. To the Wine Doctor!

(*As they are drinking the lights go down. When the lights come back on, Ahmet Beyaz, Leyla Beyaz, The Judge and The Judge's Wife are in their old places. The other characters have left the stage.*)

THE JUDGE'S WIFE: Oh, bravo! How did he do it? He must really have the ability to store tastes in his memory.

AHMET BEYAZ: Well, if I hadn't seen it with my own eyes, I wouldn't have believed it. There are hundreds of

THE GOVERNESS

	different kinds of wine. Taste any one of them and know what it is, just like that... It's **staggering!**
LEYLA BEYAZ:	And he was so shy and polite. He doesn't boast or show off at all.
AHMET BEYAZ:	I'd never seen anyone so humble.
THE JUDGE:	I really do want to meet him. You said you met him two months ago, didn't you? How did it happen?
AHMET BEYAZ:	We're exporting textiles to a company in France. The boss of that company introduced me to Orhan Gün. They were friends.
THE JUDGE:	And you'll have told him about your own collection, of course...
AHMET BEYAZ:	Well, of course! In fact, he didn't like where I was storing it and recommended the box room next to the study.
THE JUDGE:	And how many bottles do you have, Ahmet?
AHMET BEYAZ:	Well, perhaps collection is the wrong word: I've got twenty-five bottles altogether, all different years, of course, and they're all from Turkey.
THE JUDGE:	Well, I think twenty-five years is pretty impressive. So the wine doctor has been here before?
AHMET BEYAZ:	Yes, this will be his third time.
THE JUDGE:	Well, thank you for having invited us this evening.

AHMET BEYAZ:	It's we who should be thanking you. It's a real pleasure to be able to spend time with you and your wife.

(*As The Judge and The Judge's Wife are smiling, The Governess enters.*)

THE JUDGE'S WIFE:	We've heard so much about you.
THE GOVERNESS:	(*smiling*) Good things, I hope. People generally think I'm a bad-tempered, irritable woman, too, you see...
THE JUDGE:	Well, we've only ever heard good things about you. Ahmet was telling us years ago, you believe in re-incarnation, don't you?
THE GOVERNESS:	Of course. Transmigration of souls would be more accurate. There's living proof; you can see it on TV.
THE JUDGE'S WIFE:	And you say Songül's your real daughter too, don't you? I mean, not that you actually gave birth to her, Leyla did, but you're her mother, too, aren't you?
THE GOVERNESS:	Yes, something like that.
THE JUDGE:	Oh, do tell us!
THE GOVERNESS:	With pleasure, but first I have to nip into the kitchen. You both like chicken, don't you? Otherwise, we've got fish, too.
THE JUDGE:	We'd prefer chicken.
AHMET BEYAZ:	(*Interrupting*) Guvvie, the wine doctor will be arriving

THE GOVERNESS

	soon. Wouldn't you like to ask him, too?
THE GOVERNESS:	I can't possibly know what he likes or dislikes, the wino will just have to eat what he's given. (*She exits*)
AHMET BEYAZ:	You see what she's like? I don't know what I'm going to do with her.
LEYLA BEYAZ:	(*Looking at her husband sternly*) You know full well that she hasn't taken to the doctor. Leave the poor woman alone and stop harassing her!
AHMET BEYAZ:	What have I done now? The doctor's our guest, too. Don't you think she should be a bit more polite?
LEYLA BEYAZ:	Forced politeness doesn't get you anywhere. She just doesn't get on with him; that's all there is to it.
AHMET BEYAZ:	Alright, alright. You won't hear a bad word said about her, will you? Whatever she does, she's always in the right.
LEYLA BEYAZ:	For the last two months, ever since you got to know the wine doctor, your whole attitude towards her has changed. She doesn't like him; it's obvious. Is there any reason why she has to?
AHMET BEYAZ:	Look, I don't want to discuss this in front of our guests, but I've taken what you said on board. (*Turning to The Judge*) If it's OK with you, I'd like what I'm about to say not to go any further.
THE JUDGE:	There's no need to worry about that, but what

were you going to say?

AHMET BEYAZ: Why she doesn't like the wine doctor. It's obvious: she's jealous of him.

LEYLA BEYAZ: Ahmet, have you any idea what you've just said? Why on earth should she be jealous of him? What has he got to do with her?

AHMET BEYAZ: Even if everyone was as naïve as you, they still wouldn't feel the need to ask that! If Songül gets married, what will the governess do? Don't you think she'll feel she'll be out of a job?

LEYLA BEYAZ: Well, why should she! Don't you always say that her home is here? Are you saying now when Songül gets married, we'll be telling the governess to pack her bags and go?

AHMET BEYAZ: No, of course not! Quite the opposite, we'll be telling her that the house is much her home as it is ours.

LEYLA BEYAZ: Well then?

AHMET BEYAZ: Listen, let me tell you what's worrying me. It was the governess who brought up Songül; she taught her everything. Songül is her entire universe. So when she gets married and leaves home, Guvvie's going to feel abandoned. Is there any reason why she should want Songül to get married?

LEYLA BEYAZ: For God's sake, Ahmet, your imagination is running riot! You've practically cooked up a soap opera! But there's something you've forgotten and that's that she really loves Songül and always wants what's best for her more than anything else.

AHMET BEYAZ: You're quite right, but when what's best for someone you love is bad for you, you might not always want it.

LEYLA BEYAZ: Ahmet, stop all this mud-slinging! You're just wrong on this one. What, when Songül gets married, she's going to cut off all ties with us, is that what you're thinking? Take a look around! Which girls have stopped being close to their families just because they got married? Let's say she got engaged, that means looking for a house, decorating it, getting a wedding dress, sending out invitations, this, that, then she's married, and she has a baby; well, she's going to need someone to look after the baby.

AHMET BEYAZ: And what if she goes abroad? If her husband takes her off to France or somewhere?

LEYLA BEYAZ: So you're saying the wine doctor might marry our daughter and take her to Marseilles... And that's why Guvvie is angry with him and takes no notice of him... Is that what you're saying?

AHMET BEYAZ: Well, why not? You know it makes sense!

LEYLA BEYAZ: She knows very well that we'll go wherever Songül goes. You, me, the governess, we can't live without her. If she goes to Marseilles, we'll get a house over there and move. It's that simple; we've got money; we can do it; we'll even brush up on our French. Why should the governess be worried?

	She's got her own money, too; she's not dependent on us.
AHMET BEYAZ:	Yes, that's all true, but the governess can't think it through like that; she feels things like a woman.
LEYLA BEYAZ:	What? So I'm not a woman, now, am I? I think like a man, do I?
AHMET BEYAZ:	No, darling, I didn't mean it to come out like that; what I wanted to say was that she wouldn't necessarily think of those things, so she may not want Songül to get married. Love breaks all the rules.
LEYLA BEYAZ:	No, you're wrong. For the past thirty years, she's been thinking with her head, not with her heart. And she'll do whatever is in Songül's best interests, you needn't worry about that!
AHMET BEYAZ:	Well have you got any better ideas? Why do you think she won't give him the time of day?
LEYLA BEYAZ:	Why don't you ask her? I'm not going to try and guess why she doesn't like him.
AHMET BEYAZ:	You see? (*Turning to The Judge and The Judge's Wife*) Well, what do you think? Am I wrong?
THE JUDGE'S WIFE:	Well, you know, Ahmet's theory might just be right. I mean, it's hardly unheard of for love to cause jealousy... in extreme cases...
AHMET BEYAZ:	(*Turning to The Judge*) And what about you, my friend, what do you think?

THE GOVERNESS

THE JUDGE: Well, without really knowing either of them, I can't really say. And I haven't even seen this wine doctor yet. I don't know what he's like. But he'll be here soon, won't he? Give me half an hour with him, and have his character fully mapped out. And I'll tell you – more or less – why the governess hasn't taken to him.

AHMET BEYAZ: You'll analyse him with your famous "doubt everything" method, eh?

THE JUDGE: Well, if you want to analyse someone fully, you've got to sit down and talk to them. You've got to ask them all sorts of surprising questions and wear them out. Then you can get on to what you actually want to find out. Once someone's tired out and fed up, then you can get to the truth: What are they really thinking? What are their true intentions? They can't wriggle their way out with explanations.

AHMET BEYAZ: Well, I hope we'll work together one day: we could do with your experience.

THE JUDGE'S WIFE: No one can hold up a candle to him about that. He just has to sit down with someone for half an hour and he's mapped out their whole personality. And I'm not just saying that because he's my husband.

THE JUDGE: Now, Ahmet, don't you listen to a word she's saying. You've no idea how much she'd like to be rid of me! If I could just go to work, she could relax! She's trying to advertise my services.

THE JUDGE'S WIFE: Well, Your Honour, what a dreadful way to slander your faithful wife of twenty years! (*Turning to Ahmet*

	Beyaz) He really is just like how I said. And so modest, too!
AHMET BEYAZ:	Do you think I don't know that? He was even like that back at school. He was top of the class in everything. But when you spoke to him, you'd think you were talking to someone ordinary. Anyway, after the meal, we'll go to the study. I'm going to offer him a legal consultancy at our firm.
THE JUDGE:	(*To The Judge's Wife*) Say some more good things about me. Make Ahmet think there's no one else like me on the planet!
THE JUDGE'S WIFE:	But you really are like that, if I have to call a spade a spade.
LEYLA BEYAZ:	I envy the both of you. You've been friends since school. The years have passed and you still love each other so much.
THE JUDGE:	When we were young, Ahmet once did me a favour that I'll never be able to forget.
AHMET BEYAZ:	What are you talking about? It was nothing.
LEYLA BEYAZ:	That's enough of speaking in riddles; one of you should tell us.
THE JUDGE:	Well, I know Ahmet won't talk about it, so it looks like it's up to me. I was in the same class as Ahmet in grammar school. After grammar school, I registered to study law. Ahmet lost his father that year and started working in the shop. I was having a difficult time making ends meet with the money my

father was sending me every month.

LEYLA BEYAZ: So you weren't living in the same city as your father, then?

THE JUDGE: No, we're from Manisa. I was studying in Istanbul. My father would send me money every month from the village so that I could be a lawyer. Anyway, I'd got to know a girl, and we'd been going steady for two or three months. And wouldn't you know it, one day, the girl comes up to me and tells me she's pregnant!

THE JUDGE'S WIFE: Oh, aren't you just the man!

THE JUDGE: It was all in the past. It was as if my whole world came crashing down round my ears. The girl was saying if her father found out, he'd shoot both of us, and I had no idea what to do. I told her she should have an abortion. She agreed, but in those days abortion was very expensive, not to mention illegal, and where were we going to find that sort of money?

THE JUDGE'S WIFE: You could have come to me, sweetheart.

THE JUDGE: This was ten years before I'd met you. I asked everyone I knew. Well, when you're down on your luck, you soon find out who your real friends are... None of them wanted to know. They gave me all sorts of excuses, but I had nowhere left to turn, so I went to Ahmet, and he found the money and gave it to me. (*Turning to Ahmet Beyaz*) If it hadn't been for you, I'd have been finished.

THE JUDGE'S WIFE:	Well, what happened next?
THE JUDGE:	I gave her the money and never saw her again.
THE JUDGE'S WIFE:	What do you mean, you never saw her again?
THE JUDGE:	Well, maybe I should say she disappeared.
THE JUDGE'S WIFE:	Disappeared! Well, you're going to have to do better than that if you expect me to be able to understand you.
THE JUDGE:	(*To The Judge's Wife*) If you'll let me speak, I'll tell you. We'd gone to a doctor's surgery. The doctor asked me to leave her there and not to come back before five hours were up. What could I do? What could I have said? And he warned me not to wait there; after all, abortion was illegal...
THE JUDGE'S WIFE:	And after five hours, you went back and picked her up, I suppose, didn't you?
THE JUDGE:	Well, I went to collect her, but the doctor said she'd left with an oldish man. And that she hadn't wanted to go through with the abortion. I ran as fast as I could to where she was staying. According to her landlord, she'd packed up and left with an oldish man who she said was her father...
LEYLA BEYAZ:	Well what happened next?
THE JUDGE:	Like I told Ahmet back then, no matter how hard I tried, I just couldn't find her.
THE JUDGE'S WIFE:	(*To The Judge*) Well, that's just marvellous, isn't it?

THE GOVERNESS

	Do you want a boy or a girl to come knocking on our door one day and for them to run up to you and throw their arms around you saying "Hello, dad"?
THE JUDGE:	This was all thirty years ago. Maybe it was just a game to try and get some money. She knew I'd borrowed the money from Ahmet. Perhaps when she saw she wasn't going to be able to get anymore, she cut her losses and left.
THE JUDGE'S WIFE:	(*To The Judge*) Why didn't you tell me all of this before?
LEYLA BEYAZ:	(*To Ahmet Beyaz*) For pity's sake, Ahmet, why didn't you tell me about it?
AHMET BEYAZ:	Is it really that important? As far as I'm concerned, it was just a scam. (*Turning to The Judge*) And, my friend, it's not the sort of thing you should be telling women, is it? They'll start coming to all sorts of wild conclusions now.
THE JUDGE:	I've got nothing to hide. That sort of thing happens when you're a student. (*Turning to The Judge's Wife*) Darling, you didn't know me back then. And I'd completely forgotten about it, but the favour Ahmet did for me has always been at the back of my mind. And today, I suddenly remembered again.
AHMET BEYAZ:	Anyway, let's not make mountains out of mole-hills! Why don't we change the subject?
THE JUDGE'S WIFE:	Your governess wasn't like I was expecting her to

	be. Tell us a bit about her! What kind of person is she? To look at her, she seems quite sullen.
THE JUDGE:	She's been here for thirty years, hasn't she? You took her in. Why don't you tell us her life story?
AHMET BEYAZ:	You tell them, Leyla.
LEYLA BEYAZ:	You'd do a better job, Ahmet, you tell them.
AHMET BEYAZ:	But you've got a better way with words than me, Leyla dear. And you've always got your head in one of those Mills and Boon books.
THE JUDGE:	Just a minute, I can see that I'm going to have to step in. Here's my verdict: after due consideration, I have decided unanimously that Leyla Beyaz shall start the story and that when she gets tired, Ahmet Beyaz shall continue.
LEYLA BEYAZ:	Well, I suppose you can bear a punishment if it's just, here we go... So, me and Ahmet had got married. Six months later, I was pregnant. When I told him, you should have seen how happy he was. You would have thought that he was the only man in the world who had ever been an expectant father.
AHMET BEYAZ:	But isn't it natural? Isn't every prospective father like that?
THE JUDGE'S WIFE:	Well, I remember when His Honour here heard he was going to be a father: he started dancing all by himself in time to the music on the radio.
AHMET BEYAZ:	You see? It is normal.

LEYLA BEYAZ:	Ahmet, dear, of course it's normal. I was as happy as you were that day, and I was so proud – of you and of myself. It's every woman's pride to be able to give her man a child.
AHMET BEYAZ:	Anyway, carry on with the story. But when you get to the governess, let me take over, alright?
LEYLA BEYAZ:	Alright. The first two months of my pregnancy were normal, but after that, I started to feel weak. I was having bad morning sickness. The doctor ordered complete rest: I had to stay in bed all day, I wasn't to get tired, and so on...
THE JUDGE'S WIFE:	So what did you do?
LEYLA BEYAZ:	Well, when my Ahmet heard this, he hired a cook. And I had a home-help. You should have seen how those two women looked after me! I don't think many princesses have had the same care and attention as I have.
AHMET BEYAZ:	It's true! I'd call every hour on the hour to see how She was. I was so worried something might happen to her.
THE JUDGE'S WIFE:	Aaah, Ahmet, you'd better be careful or you'll end up getting struck by the evil eye if you tell anyone else things like that. Where can you find a man who's so devoted to his wife nowadays?
THE JUDGE:	(*Looking at The Judge's Wife*) I hope you're not having a dig at me...
THE JUDGE'S WIFE:	Oh, would you look at what you've just said! Have

I hit a raw nerve, darling?

AHMET BEYAZ: I can vouch for His Honour. He's very devoted to his family, too; he just doesn't show it like I do. Anyway, what do you expect? He's in the legal profession! They always try to hide their feelings...

THE JUDGE'S WIFE: I really wasn't trying to have a dig or anything. (*Looking at The Judge*) Ooh, darling, you're so touchy! You don't need to blame me for things that never even entered my mind. Anyway, you continue, Leyla.

LEYLA BEYAZ: Ahmet was so excited that he went round all the baby shops comparing prices.

AHMET BEYAZ: I'd even picked out toys. You know, Barbie dolls, lego cats and dogs, things like that.

LEYLA BEYAZ: But there was something he didn't know; I only told him after I'd had Songül and was better again. Once I knew I was pregnant, I went to a doctor someone had recommended to me. I had examinations, tests, electro, this, that, and finally he told me:

VOICE: (*The doctor*) Now look here, you shouldn't be having children. It could be very dangerous for you, even fatal. Let's terminate your pregnancy while we've still got time. I'll explain it to your husband. Remember, if you go through with it, you could die.

LEYLA BEYAZ: He told me everything in detail: I had some kind of heart problem and giving birth would be like gambling with my life. How would I ever have been able to tell Ahmet that? He wanted a child so much and couldn't wait to be a father. How was I supposed to explain? So I told the doctor I was going to keep my baby; even if I had to pay for it with my life, I was going to give my husband a child. And I told him if he said anything to Ahmet, I would kill myself. So he had to keep my secret because he was scared I might do something stupid.

THE JUDGE'S WIFE: And what happened after that? I'm dying to know...

LEYLA BEYAZ: I went into labour early. Ahmet called an ambulance to take me to hospital so I wouldn't get knocked around or jolted. I remember wearing my nightie in the ward. Then I was in intensive care for three days. At the same time, the governess had arrived here. Ahmet, dear, the rest is yours, you go on...

AHMET BEYAZ: Well, when they took Leyla into maternity, she was in a very bad way. Her face was bright purple; if you'd seen her, you'd have been afraid. There were two doctors and two nurses, and they all looked glum. You could see they were worried from the looks on their faces. All they said was:

VOICE: (*The doctor*) Mr Beyaz, could you stay in the waiting room, please? We'll hopefully be bringing you some good news soon.

AHMET BEYAZ: And what could I do? I went off to the waiting room. An hour went by, then two, and there I was, just sitting and waiting. Finally, a stoney-faced

	doctor and a stoney-faced nurse appeared.
VOICE:	(*The doctor*) Mr Beyaz, we have to inform you that your wife is in a critical condition, and we may be forced to make a terrible decision. You will have to choose which one of them you want us to save: your wife or your child.
AHMET BEYAZ:	Well, when I heard that, I started shouting at them, "What the hell are you going on about?" I think I must have passed out for a couple of minutes. Luckily for me, though, the doctor knew what he was doing.
VOICE:	(*The doctor*) Mr Beyaz, we understand you're anxious and upset, and we're doing all that we can. You don't have much time to think about it. So tell us, if we can only save one of them, which one it should be, your wife or your child? You'll have to choose and sign something.
AHMET BEYAZ:	I told them I wanted my wife. "First, I want my wife," I said, "and then our baby!" I signed the piece of paper they'd put in front of me.
THE JUDGE:	Well, what happened then?
AHMET BEYAZ:	A miracle!
VOICE:	(*The doctor*) Mr Beyaz, both of them are alive, thank God, or rather, they're still breathing. They're both in intensive care. You go home now; we'll do everything that we can.

AHMET BEYAZ: I took a taxi home; the driver asked me why I was crying, so I told him, and he had tears in his eyes, too. I took an aspirin when I got home, and I was just about to nod off when the phone rang. It was someone replying to an ad I'd put in the paper.

VOICE ON THE PHONE: (*The Governess*) I read your ad in the paper, and I know it's late to call, but a little voice inside me told me I had to. You needed a governess, well, I'd like to put myself forward...

AHMET BEYAZ: We haven't found anyone yet. My wife has just given birth and she's in intensive care. The baby's in a bad way and in intensive care, too. I don't know if they're going to pull through. What else can I say?

VOICE ON THE PHONE: Is your baby a girl?

AHMET BEYAZ: Yes, she's a girl.

VOICE ON THE PHONE: Then it must be my daughter. It's reincarnation; I got your address earlier on today from the woman who works for you. I'm on my way. (*She hangs up*)

AHMET BEYAZ: Well, I was shocked! Was this woman mad? Still, I didn't really stop to think about it and fell into a deep sleep. When I woke up, I called the clinic to see how things were.

VOICE ON THE PHONE: (*The Doctor*) We're doing everything we can, but they're still both in intensive care...

(*The lights go down. Leyla Beyaz, The Judge and The Judge's Wife stay in the background; Ahmet Beyaz is in the foreground sitting on one of the* armchairs, his head in his hands. The doorbell rings. The Governess enters with a medium-sized suitcase; she is dressed very soberly. Ahmet Beyaz stands up.)

THE GOVERNESS: We spoke on the phone, about the governess position...

AHMET BEYAZ: Yes, you're coming about the ad in the paper, aren't you? But like I said, I don't know if my wife and child are going to survive. It was a very difficult birth.

THE GOVERNESS: The child will live. And I'll bring your wife back to life. I'll give her strength. I got the name of the clinic earlier on today. I'm going there now. Don't worry about anything. I'll come back with your wife and your child. (*The Governess exits.*)

AHMET BEYAZ: She took her bag and left. I was shocked. I was wondering if she didn't have a screw loose, but she looked so normal.

LEYLA BEYAZ: Ahmet, dear, can I tell the rest of the story?

AHMET BEYAZ: Of course you can, darling, you continue.

LEYLA BEYAZ: Well, the Governess came to the clinic and spoke to the consultant, and I don't know how she managed to convince him, but they found her a nurse's uniform and she was at my bedside for three days and three nights.

AHMET BEYAZ: Tell them what she was saying while she was there, Leyla.

THE GOVERNESS

LEYLA BEYAZ: Well, when I was in intensive care in a coma, she sat on a chair next to the bed and kept talking and talking to me.

THE JUDGE'S WIFE: What, you mean while you were in a coma?

LEYLA BEYAZ: Yes, I didn't know where I was, they were keeping me alive with serum, and the Governess kept telling me:

VOICE: (*The Governess*) You'll get better, my friend, you'll come round soon, you'll open your eyes, and we'll bring our daughter in. We'll all have such a good time.

LEYLA BEYAZ: She kept repeating that to me, over and over again. The nurses at the clinic told me about it later.

THE JUDGE: Very interesting...

LEYLA BEYAZ: She went for seventy-two hours on practically no sleep. She'd go to see the baby and say some things to her, and then she'd come back to me.

AHMET BEYAZ: But that's different; it's not the same as her not wanting Songül to get married. Don't try to draw parallels between two different emotions.

LEYLA BEYAZ: Ahmet, darling, you're accusing the poor woman in the wrong. How many times do I have to tell you, the Governess hasn't got a selfish bone in her body. She loves Songül as much as she loves herself, maybe even more...

AHMET BEYAZ:	That's exactly it! It's because she loves Songül so much that she doesn't want to be separated from her. If Songül gets married, she'll go and live with her husband, and the Governess will be left hanging around like a spare part...
LEYLA BEYAZ:	There's no use talking to you! You've become obsessed with that idea!
AHMET BEYAZ:	(*Looking at The Judge and The Judge's Wife*) We're arguing about this in front of you, please forgive us. There's something I want to tell you, though. A student has joined the company, you know, one of those interns, anyway, he's studying psychology at Istanbul University. I really like chatting to him, and I learn lots of useful things from him.
LEYLA BEYAZ:	Well, I certainly hope you haven't been telling him about the Governess and Songül!
AHMET BEYAZ:	And there you have it! My own wife thinks I'm stupid! Do I really go round blabbing everything to everyone? Do you think I'm some kind of imbecile? Do you think I don't know to keep family secrets?
LEYLA BEYAZ:	Well, haven't you become touchy all of a sudden! And it's getting worse day by day. Anyway, is this intern a man? Maybe he could be...
AHMET BEYAZ:	Yes, dear, he's a man, and, no, he's not at all suitable for Songül; if you must know, he's married and has a kid.
THE JUDGE:	Well, what did this student tell you? You said you learnt lots of useful things from him...

AHMET BEYAZ: Well, every kind of behaviour has a visible side and an invisible side. They call it "conscious" and "unconscious". So if you can understand what's going on in your head, that's "conscious". And if you're affected by all sorts of things in your mind, but without you noticing, then that's "unconscious". So for example, on the one hand, of course the Governess wants Songül to get married, and she really believes that, but, on the other hand, if Songül does get married, she'll be out of a job, she's aware of that, too, and so, without being able to do anything about it, she's working against it.

LEYLA BEYAZ: Oh, well done, Ahmet! You really have hit the nail on the head there! So, on the one hand, the Governess wants Songül to get married, and on the other hand, she doesn't. And you call this psychology? Who are you trying to fool?

AHMET BEYAZ: (*Turning to The Judge*) You see? You can't tell Leyla anything. Leyla and Songül won't have a bad word said about the Governess. As far as Leyla's concerned, if it wasn't for the Governess, she wouldn't be here now, so, the Governess is always right.

LEYLA BEYAZ: Oh, Ahmet, it's not like you say! And another thing, Songül hasn't really had any real marriage opportunities so far; let's wait for one to turn up and then we'll see if you're right or not.

THE JUDGE: Ahmet, Leyla could be right, you know. Now, I'm not one for coming between husband and wife, it wouldn't be right, but I'm telling you this as a

	friend, she hasn't had any real marriage opportunities yet, so how can you judge?
AHMET BEYAZ:	But there has been someone, my friend, there has been someone, but the girl turned him down, after the Governess had poisoned her mind, of course...
LEYLA BEYAZ:	Has there? But who? Who wanted to marry Songül?
AHMET BEYAZ:	Would you just calm down and I'll tell you: the doctor, the Wine Doctor wanted to marry Songül!
LEYLA BEYAZ:	How do you know? Did he ask you for her hand?
AHMET BEYAZ:	More or less! Here's how it happened: the first time I met the Wine Doctor, I invited him to come to the factory and told him I'd be happy to see him again. Anyway, yesterday he called and showed up immediately. I thought we'd only be having a chat, but his mind was on other things...
LEYLA BEYAZ:	He asked you for Songül's hand?
AHMET BEYAZ:	Yes!
THE JUDGE'S WIFE:	Well, has he spoken to her? Have they come to some sort of agreement between themselves?
AHMET BEYAZ:	No, first he wanted my blessing and yours too. He's sure Songül will want to marry him.
LEYLA BEYAZ:	How did he open the subject? What did he say?
AHMET BEYAZ:	Well, he said it would be an honour for him to be

part of our family; apparently, we're one of the leading families in Istanbul. Because he never knew his mother and father, he feels the need – even at his age – for the love and tenderness we can provide... He seemed sincere, too...

THE JUDGE'S WIFE: (*Turning to Leyla Beyaz*) Well, Leyla, do you and Ahmet approve?

LEYLA BEYAZ: Well, I don't really know. He seems like a good man, polite and gracious. He's very measured in what he says, but there you have it: a man who knows Europe.

AHMET BEYAZ: I agree with Leyla; I mean, the man's got western culture, good manners; he not reckless like most of the youth of today.

THE JUDGE'S WIFE: And how old is he?

AHMET BEYAZ: He must be somewhere in his forties, and Songül's thirty herself, so they should get along like a house on fire. (*Turning to Leyla Beyaz*) Don't you think so, Leyla?

LEYLA BEYAZ: Well, I don't know. If it's meant to be, it'll happen... I mean, I don't think their ages are particularly well matched, but...

THE JUDGE: And, Ahmet, what did you say to your would-be son-in-law?

AHMET BEYAZ: I told him me and Leyla would be honoured. He used the word "honour", so I thought I'd use it too... But I really do think so; I mean, the man's

	got a doctorate, and doesn't that suit our family well!
LEYLA BEYAZ:	But, Ahmet, didn't you tell him that we'd have to speak to Songül first? I mean, she's the one who's going to get married, is her heart going to accept the good doctor?
AHMET BEYAZ:	What kind of father do you think I am? Of course I told him that. In fact, I was going to tell him to speak to Guvvie first; after all, if it doesn't get her seal of approval, it's not like it's going to happen, is it? I was going to say to him if he couldn't convince her, then my and Leyla's blessing would do nothing. It was on the tip of my tongue, but I somehow couldn't get it out.
LEYLA BEYAZ:	Oh, Ahmet, change the record, will you?
AHMET BEYAZ:	Look, Leyla, I'm saying this in front of our dear friends, too, and this time I'm putting my foot down. I'm not going to stand back and let the Governess get in the way of this marriage. So, Songül's come back to life, or whatever the hell it is, she's not the Governess' daughter; you gave birth to her: Songül is our daughter, the two of us. Is that clear?
LEYLA BEYAZ:	Oh, Ahmet, no one's ever claimed anything else! I mean, even the Governess herself accepts that! She just believes the soul of her little girl, who she lost in an accident, passed into Songül's body. Where's the harm in that?
AHMET BEYAZ:	As long as it doesn't stop our daughter getting

	married, then none whatsoever.
THE JUDGE'S WIFE:	I'd really like to get to know her better. She seems innocuous enough, quiet, very prim and proper.
LEYLA BEYAZ:	I'll go and call her. If I don't call her, she won't come. She's been living with us for thirty years, but she's still as polite and respectful to us as she was on the very first day. (*She exits*)
AHMET BEYAZ:	She really loves the Governess, and won't hear anything said against her.
THE JUDGE:	Well, seeing she said if it wasn't for her, she wouldn't be here today, I'd say that love has very deep roots.
AHMET BEYAZ:	You know, I really haven't got the slightest thing against her; our house is her house. No, what annoys me is her negative attitude towards the doctor. I mean, she didn't even congratulate him!
THE JUDGE:	Well, if you ask me, there must be some reason for it.
LEYLA BEYAZ:	(*Enters*) She'll be here soon; she's just checking on the chicken. Anyway, let's go into the garden, come and see the roses we've just planted.

(*They all exit together*)

Act Two

Songül enters; it is clear that she is very excited about something. Sixty seconds later, the Governess enters. It is easy to see how much she loves Songül from the expression on her face.

THE GOVERNESS: What is it, dear?

SONGÜL: I don't know where to start! You know how I'm going out with a boy, well...

THE GOVERNESS: A boy? Didn't you say he was thirty-two?

SONGÜL: God, Guvvie, it's just a figure of speech! Of course he's not a boy! He's a young man, but he's not one of those big, burly types... Anyway, he's my type.

THE GOVERNESS: Uh-huh...

SONGÜL: He's a research assistant at the moment, but next year he'll be a lecturer, and then a professor... We see each other every day, we go for long walks from the faculty building, and if it's raining, we go for a drive in his car.

THE GOVERNESS: Yes, and you go to the cinema, too.

SONGÜL: How do you know that?

THE GOVERNESS: Next time you empty your pockets, you should be more careful. Don't drop used tickets on the carpet.

THE GOVERNESS

SONGÜL: God, how could I have been so careless! Does dad know?

THE GOVERNESS: Of course not, dear. Do you think I'd tell him?

SONGÜL: Anyway, I really like him. You couldn't really call him particularly intelligent, hard-working or handsome, but I don't care. Anyway, I'm not exactly drop-dead gorgeous myself, am I?

THE GOVERNESS: For me and for your mum and dad, you're the cutest little thing in the world. And anyway, your boyfriend must think so too, if he's always going out with you.

SONGÜL: It's just that he's so shy! Oh, I don't know, how can I put it? He's very... shy.

THE GOVERNESS: You mean he hasn't even held your hand yet, let alone kiss you.

SONGÜL: God, Guvvie, how did you know that? He's completely normal; it's just he's a bit shy.

THE GOVERNESS: Look, dear, that's normal. Generally, men who devote themselves to studying or to their careers will be a bit shy with a girl.

SONGÜL: You know, Guvvie, I agree with you; it makes me feel so much better when I talk to you.

THE GOVERNESS: So, how long have you been seeing each other?

SONGÜL: In three days, it'll be two months. Don't you remember, I told you I'd started going out with him

	back in the first week. But don't tell dad because nothing's certain yet.
THE GOVERNESS:	Do you think I'd forget something like that! I meant how long have you been officially boyfriend and girlfriend?
SONGÜL:	Since yesterday. I don't know how to tell you, but I know you'll be very cross with me.
THE GOVERNESS:	No I won't. Come on, you can tell me.
SONGÜL:	Even if you don't get cross, I'm cross with myself. I've made a fool of myself.
THE GOVERNESS:	Now I'm really curious! Spit it out, then!
SONGÜL:	I met him at university. He was the friend of the husband of one of my friends. One day the four of us went somewhere together for tea. Let's meet up sometime, we said, you know, the usual... The next day he called me on my mobile. He said he couldn't get our conversation out of his head. He wanted to see my face once more. Oh, Guvvie, you should hear him! He's got such a way with words, it's impossible not to fall under his spell.
THE GOVERNESS:	Well that's great! I can't stand people who are always being crass.
SONGÜL:	Anyway, we met up the next day; the weather was beautiful, so we went for a walk. Then again the next day, Belgrade Forest, Kilyos... But I noticed he wouldn't even hold my hand. It seemed a bit odd. I'm always hearing from my friends when they go

out with boys, some of them even want to sleep with them on the first date! Sure, mine was cheerful, he laughed, he talked to me, he made jokes, but that was it! He wouldn't hold my hand, he didn't even try to kiss me, but, the thing is, I wanted him to hold my hand, I wanted him to kiss me!

THE GOVERNESS: Well, what happened yesterday?

SONGÜL: Well, I was saying to myself, I wonder if he's normal? He's not gay, is he? I mean, he doesn't look gay, or anything. It would have been obvious, and anyway, if he was gay, why would he want to go out with a girl? And I made a plan. I told him I was tired, and we sat down beneath a tree. I took his hand and put it on my breast, and then I pressed my cheek to his and kissed him on the lips. And you know, Guvvie, it all happened in a few seconds, all of this. But I regret doing it, and I feel so stupid.

THE GOVERNESS: Whatever for? Oh, but wait, first tell me what he did...

SONGÜL: Well, he was surprised. He hadn't been expecting me to do that. He moved his hand away, and for a few seconds – or maybe for a few minutes – he looked into my eyes like a child looks into its mother's eyes, and then he suddenly hugged me so tight I thought he was going to crush me. Then, like he was making up for those two wasted months, he kissed me, ah, he practically kissed the life out of me! God, it was quite a shock to the system!

THE GOVERNESS: You see, there was no need for you to worry! How did you leave each other?

SONGÜL: Well, after that, he didn't say anything; we kept on walking, hand in hand, without saying a word. He didn't even let go of my hand when we got into the car: he drove with his left hand and held mine with his other hand... He only let go of it to change gear. We could have had an accident or anything, but I didn't care! I just wanted to be able to feel his skin on mine, like it was never going to end...

THE GOVERNESS: And then?

SONGÜL: We stopped in front of a block of flats. He told me that was where he lived and invited me in. It was like I was in a dream, or I'd been hypnotised. I had all these thoughts going round and round in my head. And then, after a few minutes, one of those thoughts won, and I found myself saying, "Well, if you really want to." We climbed the stairs four, five, or however many floors there were; there was no lift. We got to the top floor out of breath. It was a tiny little flat – you know I keep going on and on about a studio flat – well, it was something like that. The bed hadn't even been made. We went inside and just sort of stared at each other; then we suddenly fell into each other's arms... Don't ask me what happened next.

THE GOVERNESS: Don't worry, I won't, not if you don't want me to.

SONGÜL: We became one, just like in those romantic films...

Or something like that. Then, would you guess what he said? "This is the first time for both of us, isn't it?" I was so mad!

THE GOVERNESS: What's there to get mad about, dear? Quite the opposite, it shows he's honest and brave. Anyway, what did you say?

SONGÜL: I said I didn't know about him, but it was my first time. And then he said maybe I'd think he was strange, but he'd gone through his whole life until then without even ever having held another girl's hand, and that I could call him cowardly and passive if I wanted, but that was just how he was. And then he told me until then there'd never been a girl who'd liked him and he'd never liked any girls; I was the first.

THE GOVERNESS: Well, that doesn't seem so bad to me; I mean, I don't think you can fault him for not being a womaniser or for not having gone out with other girls before you.

SONGÜL: But if only I'd been able to keep my big mouth shut, then everything would have been OK, but when he said that... Ah, I can't believe I said it...

THE GOVERNESS: What on earth did you say, dear?

SONGÜL: "If I'm your first, I want to be your last, too, but for that you'll have to wait for me at the altar." Oh, Guvvie, I can't tell you how stupid I feel!

THE GOVERNESS: I just can't understand you today. Why do you feel stupid? I can't see anything you've done that a normal, healthy person wouldn't do, dear.

SONGÜL: But, Guvvie, how could I sink so low?

THE GOVERNESS: What do mean, "sink so low"?

SONGÜL: You don't have to console me, you know, Guvvie. A girl should wait; the man should make the first move. But what did I do? I went meekly up to his room and seduced him, right there, in front of his bed. Oh my God, why can't I just be normal? (*She starts to cry*).

THE GOVERNESS: Don't cry. My little girl! You'll have me crying, too. Oh, my little girl! Here's where you're going wrong: you're making men out to be much more important than they really are; you're making mountains out of mole-hills. So, you wanted to sleep with a guy you really liked, that's all there is to it; there's no need to blow it up out of all proportions!

SONGÜL: That's easy enough for you to say! But it's been like that since the beginning of time...

THE GOVERNESS: Since the beginning of time? How do you know that? Is it always the man who has to make the first move when it comes to sex? Why? Come on, give me one good reason...

SONGÜL: Well, men are stronger, of course, I mean physically.

THE GOVERNESS: If by stronger you mean they can lift heavier things, then you're right. A man's muscles are more developed and so they're stronger. Look, you behaved very naturally, spontaneously...

SONGÜL: But, Guvvie, would you have done the same thing? Before marrying your future husband?

THE GOVERNESS: Yes, of course...

SONGÜL: Guvvie, you've never told me how you got married. I've asked before, but you've always changed the subject. Guvvie, tell me how you met your husband, how he persuaded you to marry him, how you got married... Tell me. I've told you everything.

THE GOVERNESS: Thank God for letting me live long enough to see this day! I'll tell you, darling, I'll tell you... Now I believe more than ever in the power of genes. Good God, it's such a relief to know we carry the same genes!

SONGÜL: I don't understand a word you're saying, Guvvie. Yes, give thanks to God, but what's that got to do with us? And more to the point, what's it got to do with genes?

THE GOVERNESS: I met my husband at school. I was a literature teacher there, and he taught history. I still remember the day we met as if it was yesterday... When we shook hands, I could hear a voice inside me going, "Don't let this one get away. He could be your husband."

SONGÜL: So, what did you do to stop him getting away?

THE GOVERNESS: At first I acted like I wasn't interested in him. Like he was just some ordinary man, what difference does it make, and I noticed that he was doing the same; it was as if he saw me as just some ordinary woman. It was then I realised it wasn't going to work: I liked him, the way he spoke, his smile, the way he stood, it all made my heart skip a beat. And I needed a husband. So I said to myself, Girl, you've got to take control, you can't expect him to do it.

SONGÜL: And what did you do next?

THE GOVERNESS: Exactly what you did thirty years later, dear!

SONGÜL: You mean you kissed him first?

THE GOVERNESS: Of course, but there's nothing to be surprised at there. He really liked going for walks. Once we'd got to know each other, we'd walk together almost every day after school. And from what I heard afterwards, the children and the teachers had started calling us the two lovebirds.

SONGÜL: Lovebirds? Were you really like that?

THE GOVERNESS: I don't know; maybe we were. There's a picnic place in Ankara called Gölbaşı. We'd have picnics there every Saturday and Sunday. And I realised we were a pair of lovebirds, but only in appearance. So one day I took his hand and pressed it against my breast...

SONGÜL: Just like I did! You did exactly the same as me! And then did you kiss him?

THE GOVERNESS: Of course I did.

THE GOVERNESS

SONGÜL: And what did you say to him after you'd kissed him?

THE GOVERNESS: "Don't think any the worse of me," I said, "We've been going out for a month now, and I really like you. That's why I kissed you, and if you like me, too, then let's dot the i's and cross the t's."

SONGÜL: Did you really say that, Guvvie, "dot the i's and cross the t's"?

THE GOVERNESS: Yes, that's exactly what I said: "dot the i's and cross the t's."

SONGÜL: And what did he do?

THE GOVERNESS: "Let's dot them and cross them, then," that's what he said.

SONGÜL: Well, it's not exactly romantic, but I suppose it's realistic, at least. Anyway, what happened next?

THE GOVERNESS: He told me he was going to tell his mother and father and then ask for my hand.

SONGÜL: What? Was that it?

THE GOVERNESS: What else do you want? That was enough for me. I really liked him, and I think it was something more than just fancying him. I desired him, too.

SONGÜL: And you proposed to him. I told Erol to wait for me at the altar; you said dot the i's and cross the t's. They both mean the same thing, don't they?

THE GOVERNESS:	Of course they do; they both mean the same thing. So don't be so hard on yourself. What you did yesterday was what I had done years before.
SONGÜL:	I'm not upset anymore. Anyway, what happened after that?
THE GOVERNESS:	Both our families got together and we celebrated. The men drank rakı and the women drank lemonade. And two months later, we tied the knot.
SONGÜL:	Why were the men drinking rakı and the women, lemonade? Are women second class citizens or something?
THE GOVERNESS:	OK, OK, I see, you're a feminist, but don't shoot everything that moves. If they'd wanted to, the women could have drunk rakı, too. No one was stopping them.
SONGÜL:	Anyway, how was the wedding? We're there lots of people?
THE GOVERNESS:	It was a simple family affair. Ah but... Guess who came to the church that day... only the classes me and my husband taught! Imagine, hundreds of pupils with colourful cards wishing us love, luck and happiness. Ah, brightly coloured and in all the shapes and sizes you can imagine... I was overwhelmed by it all and started crying.
SONGÜL:	Oh, Guvvie, what a magical sight! Sometimes I say to myself I should be a teacher, too, and be like a mother to hundreds of children, or even thousands. But how did the children get there; I mean, wasn't

THE GOVERNESS

                        the headmaster cross with them?

THE GOVERNESS: The headmaster gave me away. And the deputy head was the best man. There must have been about a quarter of the school there; we were surprised! Of course, they were there without permission, but thankfully there wasn't an accident or anything. Of course, the headmaster pretended to be very cross with them and gave them a good telling off the next day, "If you ever do that again, blah blah blah..."

SONGÜL: But, Guvvie, do you ever miss those days, when you were a teacher?

THE GOVERNESS: No, I don't.

SONGÜL: There's one thing I'm really sorry about, Guvvie. I know you never remarried because of me.

THE GOVERNESS: And where on earth did you get that idea into your head?

SONGÜL: Mum told me, and she warned me not to talk to you about it, not to open up old wounds.

THE GOVERNESS: Well, let me continue telling you my life story, then. I got pregnant a few months after getting married, and we had a baby girl. We called her Gülçin. We were so happy... I'd stopped teaching to look after her... And then there was the accident... Gülçin was only seven days old... It was a Sunday, a glorious Sunday, and we thought we'd go out so she could get some fresh air. We had a little car, and so we got in. I was driving. My husband was in the back holding her... The accident... There was a lorry... it's brakes failed and it ran into the back of us. My husband and Gülçin were killed instantly. They took me to hospital, but I didn't have a scratch... God hadn't seen fit to call me to his side... (*She starts to cry*)

SONGÜL: Guvvie, please don't go on.

THE GOVERNESS: As soon as I'd got over the shock and come round, I told the nurse to bring Gülçin to me, she must be hungry and I had to feed her. Then I asked where my husband was and said I really missed him.

SONGÜL: Guvvie, please don't cry, I'm such a bad person for making you remember all of this.

THE GOVERNESS: Don't be silly, dear, it's better like this; it's good for all the sadness that's been welling up inside me all these years to come out as tears. They discharged me the same day. I couldn't stay in Ankara any longer. I came to stay with a relative in Istanbul. The next day I saw an ad in the paper looking for a governess for a newborn baby, and I immediately applied. Your father had placed the ad. And ever since then, I've been here...

SONGÜL: And you never remarried because of me. Because if you'd got married, you'd have had to go and you wouldn't have been able to look after me and bring me up.

THE GOVERNESS: Well, I know I did the right thing. I don't regret it even for one moment. Now, tell me, why did you bring up the subject?

SONGÜL: You didn't actually give birth to me, but you really have been a mother to me. As a family, we'll never be able to repay you for all you've done. You know, Guvvie, if I get married one day, obviously I'll move out and go and live with my husband. But you come with us, OK? Without you it would be so dull and horrible.

THE GOVERNESS: Oh, you're such a child! My dear, a husband and wife need time to themselves. Yes, I lived with your mother and father, but that was different, and we'll talk about that some other time. I promise. Now, you go and get changed; you know your father doesn't want you meeting the guests dressed in jeans. And don't be sad! Go and get changed, now, and go to your father.

SONGÜL: OK, but there's one more thing I want to ask you. Answer and I'll immediately go and put my best frock on.

THE GOVERNESS: Come on then, let's hear it.

SONGÜL: (*Opening her arms as wide as she can*) Guvvie, why do I love you this much! (*She goes and hugs The Governess*)

THE GOVERNESS: Off you go, my girl, or else I really won't be able to hold myself back and I'll start crying again.

(*Songül exits; The Governess remains*)

Ahmet and Leyla Beyaz enter with The Judge and The Judge's Wife.

THE JUDGE'S WIFE: May we call you Guvvie? I think even Leyla and

Ahmet have forgotten your real name!

THE GOVERNESS: (*Turning to Ahmet and Leyla Beyaz*) Well? Let's see if you can remember my name as it stands on my birth certificate?

AHMET BEYAZ: Ooh, give me a moment, I'll have to think about that... It was Emel, wasn't it?

THE GOVERNESS: Yes, Mr Beyaz, you got it straight away, Emel Deniz... But because even the grocer and the butcher call me Guvvie, even I sometimes have difficulty remembering my real name.

THE JUDGE: Well then, after due consideration, Miss Emel Deniz shall hereafter be known as Guvvie by a unanimous decision.

THE GOVERNESS: Well, if that's how the court has decided, we have no choice but to accept its judgement.

THE JUDGE'S WIFE: Guvvie, I hear you believe we come back to earth after death. We carry on living... And it's something that really interests me, could you tell me more?

THE GOVERNESS: Of course, where can I begin, now? Well, after your physical death, your soul roams for a while looking for somewhere it can take rest and shelter. Of course, it follows from that that the soul is immortal. When your heart stops through illness, an accident, old age or whatever, and when your brain functioning stops, your soul leaves your body and looks for a new home.

THE JUDGE'S WIFE: OK, but when your soul is looking for a new home,

	can it pass into a plant or an animal that's waiting to be born?
THE GOVERNESS:	Or, indeed, the opposite could happen. The soul of a plant or of an animal could enter a human body.
THE JUDGE:	They call it "transmigration of souls", don't they? But anyway, how long does it last? Forever?
THE GOVERNESS:	We could say forever. There's nothing after eternity...
THE JUDGE:	Well, when does this transmigration of souls end?
THE GOVERNESS:	Once the soul has attained perfect passivity, it stops roaming and is reunited with God.
THE JUDGE'S WIFE:	Your Honour, please don't get lost in the depths of philosophy, and don't drag us down with you... we were having a pleasant conversation here!
THE JUDGE:	Alright then, but I'd like to continue this conversation with Guvvie another day.
THE GOVERNESS:	With pleasure!
AHMET BEYAZ:	Oh, I've just thought of something! You know how you can say someone's catty? Well, maybe it means that a stray cat was dying, and it's soul entered the body of a girl who was being born at the time, and when she grew up, she had the personality of a stray cat.
LEYLA BEYAZ:	Oh, yes, or like when we say he's as thick as two short planks, it might be that a tree was being cut

down – plants have souls too, after all – and its soul took nest in a baby.

AHMET BEYAZ: There are so many examples, like...

LEYLA BEYAZ: ...like if a snake is dying and its soul escapes from its body and escapes to a baby who's being born. When the baby grows up, he'll be a real snake in the grass...

AHMET BEYAZ: ...and everyone will be sick of him.

(*Orhan Gün, otherwise known as The Wine Doctor, enters. Everyone rises to their feet and shake hands with him.*)

THE JUDGE: Ah, Mr Gün, I'm so grateful to Ahmet and Leyla that they've given us the opportunity of meeting you. I've read so much about you in the papers. You have a very colourful personality. That luxury mansion you inherited, your dispute with a French hospital, receiving the title of doctor... How did it all happen?

THE WINE DOCTOR: Well, it was a great honour for me when Mr Beyaz told me he was going to introduce me to a retired judge and his wife. I don't really know anybody here, but Mr Beyaz has driven away my loneliness and introduced me to some of the most distinguished people in the country, so really, it's me who should be saying thank you.

AHMET BEYAZ: Well, I call Orhan "doctor", don't I? But, I mean, if the French newspapers have seen fit to call him that...

THE GOVERNESS

THE WINE DOCTOR: To be with people who appreciate quality, people who are quality themselves... I can't tell you how happy I am. May I think of you all as friends?

THE JUDGE: But, of course!

AHMET BEYAZ: We'd be honoured!

THE JUDGE: And what's your life story?

THE WINE DOCTOR: Well, my friends, there isn't really very much to tell... I've always kept my nose to the grind stone, trying to make something of my life ...

AHMET BEYAZ: Well, it looks like you already have, and it's not just me saying that: the French newspapers are singing your praises too.

LEYLA BEYAZ: It makes me feel so proud! Let them see what we're made of!

THE WINE DOCTOR: I was born in Istanbul, and I must have been about five when I lost my father, and then three years later, I lost my mother.

AHMET BEYAZ: So unfortunate...

THE JUDGE'S WIFE: Who can ever know what kind of hole that left in your heart?

THE WINE DOCTOR: You're right, when you've got no one left to hold your hand, you've got to be strong by yourself if you want to overcome all the obstacles in your life. I realised that when I was eight...

AHMET BEYAZ:	I've also had to struggle in life, but that didn't start until I was twenty... My dear friend, I congratulate you.
THE JUDGE:	And what did your father do, Mr Gün?
THE WINE DOCTOR:	We had a small corner shop. After my father passed away, my mother kept it going on her own for two years.
THE JUDGE:	And what happened to the shop after you lost your mother?
THE WINE DOCTOR:	A relative came and sold the shop. First, he paid of the hospital and doctors' bills, but of course, that was like a small fortune to us. With what was left, they bought me some clothes and gave me a few hundred francs as I was on my way to Marseilles.
THE JUDGE:	You were an only child, weren't you?
THE WINE DOCTOR:	Yes, that's right.
THE JUDGE:	And how did you end up in Marseilles?
THE WINE DOCTOR:	Well, you see, because there was no one to look after me in Istanbul, and my uncle lived in Marseilles, they wrote to him and, I mean, what else could he do? He wrote back saying send him over. His wife was French and they had two boys.
LEYLA BEYAZ:	You must have been really afraid stepping on to the plane.
THE WINE DOCTOR:	Plane? They put me on the train! And for three

days and four nights, I was in absolute terror – what if my uncle doesn't come and pick me up from the station!

LEYLA BEYAZ: And is that what happened?

THE WINE DOCTOR: Oh, didn't it just!

THE JUDGE'S WIFE: Ooh, tell us about that, too!

THE WINE DOCTOR: My mother's cousin had given me a good drilling in what I had to do on the train, and he'd told the conductor, too.

LEYLA BEYAZ: Well, that's good; they do the same thing on planes, too: they tell the hostesses.

THE WINE DOCTOR: Well, anyway, I finally arrived in Marseilles. The French conductor tried talking to me in French, and I was trying to speak Turkish to him. He didn't understand a word I was saying, and I didn't understand a word he was saying; we had to make do with sign language.

LEYLA BEYAZ: What a thing to have to go through, and at that age!

THE WINE DOCTOR: Well, anyway, at the railway station in Marseilles, the conductor took me by the hand and led me off the train. We look around, but no one had come to meet me. I started crying my eyes out. And I mean, what could the conductor do? He tried to console me with gestures and sign language. But the time was getting on, and the man had a job to do, he couldn't wait any longer, so he took me to the police station and left me there.

THE JUDGE'S WIFE: And how did the police treat you?

THE WINE DOCTOR: Oh, they were very good to me. I remember it like it was yesterday: they gave me orange juice and chocolate to get me to stop crying, and then they looked in my bag to see who I was from my passport, and then they were going to call the Turkish consulate, I think. There was a policewoman. To keep me entertained, she drew a picture of a little girl. It think it was her own daughter. Then she drew another picture next to it: a handsome man. He must have been her husband. I stopped crying and started to smile. She made me stand up and hugged me, and suddenly I remembered my mother – she used to do the same; she would hug me whenever I cried.

LEYLA BEYAZ: Now that's what I'd call good people.

THE WINE DOCTOR: When the policewoman hugged me, I did what I used to do to my mother. I kissed her hand, and when the police saw me do that, they all clapped. I felt very pleased with myself, but of course, it made me blush, too.

AHMET BEYAZ: I think it's wonderful you can remember all of that after all these years.

THE WINE DOCTOR: You never forget those things that stir up strong emotions in you, even years later.

THE JUDGE: And why had your uncle gone to Marseilles?

THE WINE DOCTOR:	Well, when he left school, he found a job over there in a Turkish company, fell in love and got married.
AHMET BEYAZ:	And you lived with them, didn't you? How did your stepmother treat you?
THE WINE DOCTOR:	Oh, she was a very good person. But what was the poor woman supposed to do? She was a cashier in a supermarket. She'd go to work at the crack of dawn, and she'd come home in the evenings completely worn out. My uncle was the same; he was a technician in an electronics factory. They had difficulty making ends meet with the money they were on. I stayed with them for two years.
LEYLA BEYAZ:	You must have lived through some hard times ...
THE WINE DOCTOR:	Yes, I really have. Many unhappy times. Once one of my cousins told me I was the reason they had money problems, and that if it hadn't been for me, what their mother and father made would have been more than enough to see them through. Those words crushed me. Yes, many unhappy times... My cousins were jealous of me, and they'd gang up on me and beat me up. When my uncle saw things weren't working out, he sent me to an orphanage. I was ten.
THE JUDGE:	And, well, how did you learn French? Did you have any trouble?
THE WINE DOCTOR:	Well, it sort of happened all by itself, plus I really liked the language, and I tried my best to speak well when I was in the orphanage.

LEYLA BEYAZ:	But your Turkish is really good, too. How come you didn't forget it?
THE WINE DOCTOR:	My uncle would always speak to me in Turkish. And I was lucky at school: I had a Turkish friend. Just to spite the other children, we'd speak Turkish amongst ourselves. He'd go to Istanbul every holiday and bring me back lots of books in Turkish. So I'd read them, and I'd sometimes even read the ones I liked more than once.
LEYLA BEYAZ:	If you'd like, I can give you some Turkish novels. We've got so many of them lying around here!
AHMET BEYAZ:	Leyla! The doctor is a serious man! You don't really think he's going to want to read your Mills and Boon novels, now, do you?
LEYLA BEYAZ:	(*Giving her husband a harsh look*) What? Are you saying I'm not a serious person just because I read that type of book? No, don't interrupt me! Can you tell how serious someone is just from the books they read? You know there are some people who puff themselves up and won't read that kind of novel, but most of them either don't read at all or else read very very little. OK? They're just would-be intellectuals, OK?
AHMET BEYAZ:	Come on, Leyla darling, there's no need to fly off the handle. All I wanted to say was, I mean, some people might not have so much time on their hands.
LEYLA BEYAZ:	I know exactly what you wanted to say, Ahmet. Anyway, let's drop it.

THE GOVERNESS

THE WINE DOCTOR:	Mrs Beyaz, if you could lend me a few of your books after dinner... I don't really have anything to read this evening, you see...
LEYLA BEYAZ:	But of course, I'd be happy to!
THE JUDGE:	Anyway, how long did you stay at the orphanage?
THE WINE DOCTOR:	Until I left school. And after that, I didn't want to study anymore; I wanted to earn some money.
THE JUDGE'S WIFE:	So you got into the wine business after leaving school?
THE WINE DOCTOR:	Well, at high school, actually, even when I was still at middle school, the orphanage would find me a job for the summer holidays. At a winery, of all places... And I really loved the work, and, in a short space of time, I'd become quite successful.
THE JUDGE:	And what exactly did you do there?
THE WINE DOCTOR:	Well at first it was just donkey work, but with time, they gave me more important things to do.
THE JUDGE:	Really? Like what?
THE WINE DOCTOR:	Well, for example, tasting the wine to check its quality. Now, they do have laboratory machines to do the same thing, but it's not the same. You have to take the human element into account...
THE JUDGE:	Oh, you're quite right. You should never underestimate the personal touch. It's wrong to trust machines and gadgets one hundred percent for

	everything...
THE WINE DOCTOR:	Well, quite, but, it's a pity that people who think like us are beginning to be in the minority.
THE JUDGE:	And so, my friend, how did you get this title of "wine doctor"?
THE WINE DOCTOR:	Well, a few months ago the Marseilles Wine Federation held a competition. We had to taste different wines and say which year and which region they were from. Lots of people entered, so did I. I had the fewest minus points, so I came first. And because of that, their newsletter gave me the title "le docteur du vin". And that's all there is to it...
AHMET BEYAZ:	But you're so modest about the whole thing! I don't imagine it's easy to win a title like that.
THE JUDGE:	Do they award it every year?
THE WINE DOCTOR:	Well, I don't know. This year was the first, so maybe they'll start awarding it from now on.
AHMET BEYAZ:	I mean, it's not like they should only call people who've been to medical school doctors, now, is it? You've got doctors of law, doctors of economics, and now there's a new one to join their ranks, "wine doctor"...
THE JUDGE:	Ahmet told us how you tasted some wine here and knew what its year and region were. We were just talking about it, actually, before you came.
THE WINE DOCTOR:	Oh, it was a very simple test... It's not even worth

talking about.

LEYLA BEYAZ: There's no need to be so modest, dear, you knew what it was just like that...

AHMET BEYAZ: Well, doctor, what do you say? Would you like to take another test like last time?

THE WINE DOCTOR: Why not? I'm ready.

AHMET BEYAZ: But you know, this time it might be very hard, you might not know the answer...

THE WINE DOCTOR: Well, like they say, you've got to put your money where your mouth is. And I shall.

AHMET BEYAZ: Well, in that case, let's invite the good doctor to a test like that before dinner.

THE WINE DOCTOR: I'm at your service.

AHMET BEYAZ: Ah, you flatter us...

THE JUDGE: Well, before we enter our friend into an exam he'll no doubt pass, I'd like to touch on something that was in the papers...

THE WINE DOCTOR: Be my guest!

THE JUDGE: You had some sort of disagreement with a hospital in Marseilles and took them to court, I think, now what was that all about?

THE WINE DOCTOR: Yes, that's right, I am taking one of them to court. I was telling you about my uncle. Well, he'd got a

	weak heart...
THE JUDGE:	I'm sorry to interrupt you, but this uncle, he's the same one who looked after you in Marseilles, isn't he?
THE WINE DOCTOR:	Yes, he is. Anyway, I always really liked him and his wife. We lost her in a car accident the year I left school. My uncle was devastated. He'd always had a weak heart, anyway, and now he started to live on his own.
LEYLA BEYAZ:	But he had two sons, didn't he? Didn't they look after their father?
THE WINE DOCTOR:	Well, I'm afraid my two cousins were hardly dutiful sons. When their mother passed away, they were both in America. They didn't even come to the funeral.
THE JUDGE'S WIFE:	I don't know, you work your fingers to the bone for them only for them not to be there the day you're buried.
THE JUDGE:	What difference does it make if they're there or not! You heard what the governess said, souls change places. You'll see, one day we'll be caught up in the stress of finding another body, and we won't even notice who was there and who wasn't.
THE JUDGE'S WIFE:	Well, I don't know about that; all I know is that I want my children to carry my coffin when I'm dead.
THE JUDGE:	Well, you'll have to tell them yourself, then. (*Turning*

THE GOVERNESS

	to the Wine Doctor) Let's carry on from where we left off, now, what was this court case the papers were mentioning?
THE WINE DOCTOR:	Well, one teatime my uncle had a sudden heart attack. The neighbours took him to hospital. The usual doctor was off that day, so another doctor examined him and decided he needed an operation. Because I was his only relative, they found me that day from his mobile phone and wanted my consent. I mean, what could I have said apart from do everything you have to?
AHMET BEYAZ:	You said the right thing, my friend.
THE WINE DOCTOR:	Anyway, they hastily operated on him, but unfortunately, they couldn't save him.
LEYLA BEYAZ:	God rest his soul! I can't begin to imagine how upset you must have been!
THE WINE DOCTOR:	Of course, I was really shaken by that loss because he had been a father to me, as well as an uncle...
THE JUDGE:	Well, anyway, what's the court case about?
THE WINE DOCTOR:	Well, the hospital sent me a rather hefty bill, you know, for the operation, the tests, the drugs and all that.
AHMET BEYAZ:	And you're contesting it, aren't you?
THE WINE DOCTOR:	Of course I am! I sent them a letter telling them I wouldn't be paying.

THE JUDGE:	And what grounds do you have for not paying?
THE WINE DOCTOR:	Well, I wrote saying that my uncle had had many heart attacks and they'd never wanted to operate on him before and that the doctor who did decide to operate was wrong, and so I wasn't going to give them a single franc.
THE JUDGE:	And what did they say?
THE WINE DOCTOR:	Someone called me from the accounts department of the hospital to tell me if I didn't pay they'd be taking legal action against me.
LEYLA BEYAZ:	And what did you say?
THE WINE DOCTOR:	Well, I told them I wasn't going to give them a single franc and I yelled down the phone, "You killed my uncle!"
AHMET BEYAZ:	Weren't you afraid to make that kind of accusation?
THE WINE DOCTOR:	What have I got to be afraid of? If I'm wrong, they can prove it in court!
THE JUDGE:	And, well, what happened next?
THE WINE DOCTOR:	The administrative board of the hospital met, and they invited me to attend, too. And I told them, all I ask is that you answer me this: if you have an electrical problem in your house, you call an electrician; the electrician fixes the problem and you pay him, don't you? But what if he can't fix it? What if he can't bring light to your house? What then? You don't pay!

And I gave them another example: I told them if you get in a taxi and you've told the driver where you want to go, and if you have an accident on the way and you can't get to where you want to go, do you still pay the taxi fare? Of course not!

And another one. If one of your relatives gets on a plane and the plane crashes, and if the ticket is from a travel agency, do the heirs pay the agency for the ticket? Of course not!

Then, members of the board, I said, you are wrong in wanting this money. Had my uncle survived, then of course I would have paid, right down to the last centime.'

THE JUDGE:	And how did they reply to that?
THE WINE DOCTOR:	They said they'd got permission from me before the operation and that no heart operation had a one hundred percent survival rate. They said I shouldn't use my uncle's death as an excuse not to pay.
AHMET BEYAZ:	Well, how did the dispute end?
THE WINE DOCTOR:	The told me they'd sue and get the money from me down to the last franc.
LEYLA BEYAZ:	And what did you say then?
THE WINE DOCTOR:	"Just you try!" I said, and I told them if they tried suing me, I'd be suing the hospital and the doctor who performed the wrong operation.
THE JUDGE'S WIFE:	You do have the right to do that, don't you? I

	mean, have you seen a lawyer about it?
THE WINE DOCTOR:	No, not yet because I haven't received a summons yet. Oh, before I forget, I also said I'd take them to the European Court of Human Rights.
THE JUDGE'S WIFE:	Why not in France? Why somewhere else?
THE WINE DOCTOR:	They asked me the same thing and asked me if I didn't trust the French legal system. So I told them of course I trusted it, but it was just that the judge would be a legal specialist, not a medical one, so what would he do? He'd ask a panel of experts if the doctor's decision to operate had been correct or not, and I didn't want the experts to be French doctors.
LEYLA BEYAZ:	But why not? Aren't French doctors very good?
THE WINE DOCTOR:	I'm not qualified to judge, but what I can say is this: the French stick together. I doubt very much if French doctors would be neutral. The best thing is to ask doctors and judges from some other country.
LEYLA BEYAZ:	You know best, I suppose, after all, you studied in France, grew up there and made a name for yourself there, but won't your behaviour offend them? I mean, won't they get upset?
THE WINE DOCTOR:	Look, I've got a French passport, and of course, I love France very much, but justice is justice. We shouldn't forget: first law and justice, then love for a country. That's what I believe, at any rate...

THE GOVERNESS

THE JUDGE: And from what I've read in the papers, it looks like the doctors have come out against you being awarded the title of "wine doctor". They even said it was ridiculous. Now, it was the Marseilles Wine Federation that gave you the title, wasn't it?

THE WINE DOCTOR: Well, they can say what they like! I don't even know what to call their nonsense! They put on their white coats and think they're better than everyone else. They're untouchable. That's just what they're like; don't worry about it.

AHMET BEYAZ: Well, like I said, you've doctors of economics and doctors of law, so why on earth not a wine doctor. If only you'd said that too...

THE WINE DOCTOR: You know, it's a shame I didn't. I just told them I wasn't the person they should be talking to, and that they should go and complain to the Marseilles Wine Federation.

THE JUDGE'S WIFE: And what did they have to say to that?

THE WINE DOCTOR: It was someone from the French Medical Union, and you'll never believe what he said!

LEYLA BEYAZ: Well, don't keep us in suspense, what did he say?

THE WINE DOCTOR: "Well, if we can find anyone from your Federation who's sober, then we will!"

AHMET BEYAZ: Well, the cheek of it! It's pure insolence! I mean, the nerve, saying everyone in the Federation is drunk!

THE WINE DOCTOR:	Oh, the French just love their wit. They'll try and say something witty at every opportunity; it's a sign of intelligence. And they always like to show how clever they are.
AHMET BEYAZ:	Well said, my friend, well said!
THE JUDGE:	So what happened in the end?
THE WINE DOCTOR:	Well, I asked the person on the other end of the phone exactly who he thought was going to pay any attention to him. And you won't believe the answer he came back with!
THE JUDGE:	What did he say?
AHMET BEYAZ:	"Just you wait til you get sick and then we'll see how much attention you pay me!"
THE JUDGE:	Well, it's hardly very pleasant; in fact, it's downright vulgar.
THE WINE DOCTOR:	Well, they started it. Apparently I'm not good enough for the title of doctor. It would appear that wine is not as deep a subject as law or economics. Who ever heard of such a thing? A wine doctor!
THE JUDGE:	And I take it they know about your dispute with the hospital?
THE WINE DOCTOR:	Oh, they're unrelated...
AHMET BEYAZ:	(*To The Judge*) My friend, in this case we've got a patient who dies under the knife and an heir who, believing the doctor to be responsible for the

death, refuses to pay for the medication, the care and the operation. If you were the judge, what would your verdict have been?

THE JUDGE: I don't know all the ins and outs of French law. It's a different country, after all, but it's like this: who will show that the doctor who performed the operation really was negligent or not, and how? If the court pronounces in favour of the wine doctor, it could open the floodgates, and then the medical establishment would suffer an undeserved blow. Just imagine what would happen if everyone took legal action whenever a patient died on the operating table...

THE JUDGE'S WIFE: You're might be retired, but have you forgotten all your legal notions? It was you, wasn't it, who said that the law was for the people? I mean, what if the surgeon really was negligent, why should the wine doctor pay?

THE JUDGE: Now, darling, don't immediately fly off the handle! Who's going to prove it, and how?

THE JUDGE'S WIFE: How should I know? They should bring intelligent people together, and they should resolve the problem.

THE JUDGE: And who might these intelligent people be? If you give us their addresses, we can go and find them.

THE JUDGE'S WIFE: That's what you should be thinking about! But, as an example, doctors and lawyers could come and put their heads together.

AHMET BEYAZ: Now, there's something here that I just can't get my head around. Let me tell you. One of my friends went deaf, and the doctor said he should have an operation, so he did. For a few months afterwards, it looked like he'd got better, and then he realised that the operation had made no difference; he still couldn't hear.

LEYLA BEYAZ: Ah yes, and on top of that his financial situation wasn't exactly what you'd call glittering, either. And it wasn't like what he paid to the doctor and the hospital was some sort of symbolic sum, I mean, it blew a big hole in his budget. It's crying shame if you ask me...

AHMET BEYAZ: Now, it'd be different if he really had got better and if nothing bad had happened to him.

THE WINE DOCTOR: Let me say something: suppose you've got a court case and you go to a lawyer, well, you can come to an agreement where if you win, you pay the lawyer so much, and if you lose, you pay much less.

AHMET BEYAZ: Yes, that's exactly what I wanted to say. If the patient doesn't get better, he could pay less or get his money back. And if the patient dies, he wouldn't have to pay at all.

THE JUDGE: Now, look, my friends, it's easy to talk, but it's not as easy as you think.

THE JUDGE'S WIFE: Exactly, darling! You said it wasn't easy, but you didn't say impossible. So that means it must be possible to come up with laws to protect patients and their next of kin. What if you class patients as

	consumers?
THE JUDGE:	But what do they consume?
THE JUDGE'S WIFE:	Their health and their wealth, isn't that enough for you?
THE WINE DOCTOR:	Well, friends, it gives me such joy to see that on this subject everyone – with the exception of the judge – takes my side. That makes me feel even more comfortable among you.
AHMET BEYAZ:	Just a minute! We haven't heard anything from the Governess! She's just been listening. (*Turning to the Wine Doctor*) Why don't you ask her what she thinks?
THE WINE DOCTOR:	Well, what do you think?
THE GOVERNESS:	I think that the judge is right.
THE WINE DOCTOR:	(*Trying to hide his irritation with the Governess*) And where is Miss Beyaz? I would have liked to see her take my side.
AHMET BEYAZ:	She'll be down in a moment.

(*Songül enters wearing a smart blouse and skirt. She hugs the Judge and The Judge's Wife. She shakes the Wine Doctor's hand coldly, trying not to make eye contact. The Governess and Ahmet Beyaz look at Songül lovingly*)

AHMET BEYAZ:	Well, we've had a friendly exchange of views, but let's leave the rest up to the lawyers and doctors. Now we can start our meal, prepared under the

	watchful eye of the Governess, but first, what do you say, shall we have a little bet with the good doctor, like we did last time?
THE WINE DOCTOR:	I'd be honoured.
AHMET BEYAZ:	Now, I've already told you about the bet I had with the good doctor a month ago. He knew the year and the region of the wine we put before him. We'll have another bet today. Just for a bit of fun...
THE WINE DOCTOR:	I'm ready, Mr Beyaz.
AHMET BEYAZ:	OK, my friend, now the wine I'm going to put before you today is not something that you'll easily guess. You're going to lose. So, be prepared for that, and, whatever you do, don't take it to heart. I mean, it's only a bit of fun, after all!
THE WINE DOCTOR:	I wouldn't be so sure of that! You'll see, I'll win again.
AHMET BEYAZ:	Oh this isn't something that's probably impossible, oh no, this one's definitely impossible. One thousand five hundred percent I win.
THE WINE DOCTOR:	What did I say before? You've got to put your money where your mouth is.
AHMET BEYAZ:	Look, my friend, if I'm speaking so confidently, it must mean that I know something, mustn't it?
THE WINE DOCTOR:	Of course, I'm sure you know many things, but there are also things you don't know.

AHMET BEYAZ:	And what might they be, I wonder?
THE WINE DOCTOR:	My talent. You underestimate me.
AHMET BEYAZ:	Ah, but, listen, today's wine is a Turkish wine, I mean, sure, if we were talking about a French wine, you might know, that's were you're from, after all, but we're not...
THE WINE DOCTOR:	When I was in Marseilles, I found time to try Turkish wines, too. I'm no stranger to what my country produces!
AHMET BEYAZ:	No, I'm sure you're not, but this is from somewhere where no one would ever think of.
THE WINE DOCTOR:	Well, you know, it's upsetting that you don't believe in the powers I've had since birth.
AHMET BEYAZ:	Far from it, my friend, far from it! But it's like the saying goes, "You've made your bed, so you must lie on it!"
THE WINE DOCTOR:	But, remember, there's another saying: "Expect the unexpected!"
AHMET BEYAZ:	Anyway, what are we playing for? What about a silk shirt? (*Laughing*) I mean, I'm going to win anyway, and I don't want you having to owe me too much!
THE WINE DOCTOR:	What? You want to play for something that small! I don't think so... I think we should take it a little more seriously and bet something a little more, ahem, realistic...

AHMET BEYAZ:	But, my friend, last time, in this very house, at this very table, you guessed the region and the year correctly, but this time round, the wine is much more mysterious, an enigma, even, and I wouldn't be able to sleep at night if I thought I'd made you spend a lot of money.
THE WINE DOCTOR:	Oh, I wouldn't worry about not getting enough beauty sleep, Mr Beyaz! You're going to lose, and I'll certainly have no trouble getting to sleep!
AHMET BEYAZ:	Well, you can't say I didn't warn you. Anyway, what do you want to bet?
THE WINE DOCTOR:	Something very precious to me... Ever since I came to this house, the thing that's the most precious to me...
LEYLA BEYAZ:	We're all dying to know! What is it?
THE WINE DOCTOR:	First, I'll tell you what I'll give if I lose, and then, what I'll get if I win...
AHMET BEYAZ:	Well, come on then, spit it out!
THE WINE DOCTOR:	If I lose, I'll give you my mansion, the one that the newspapers can't praise enough, my inheritance...
LEYLA BEYAZ:	You're crazy; it's a joke, it must be!
AHMET BEYAZ:	Now, we all like a joke, my friend. Forgive Leyla's little outburst, she just got a bit overexcited, that's all.
LEYLA BEYAZ:	That's right, I just blurted it out... you suggested it

	in such an excentric way!
THE WINE DOCTOR:	Well, we're all friends here, so I've got no reason to take exception to the word "crazy", now do I?
THE JUDGE'S WIFE:	OK, well you've told us what you'll give if you lose, but what will Ahmet give you if you win?
THE WINE DOCTOR:	Nothing. I'm not going to ask for any of Mr Beyaz' property...
AHMET BEYAZ:	Just a minute, what's that supposed to mean? Is there something I've missed?
THE WINE DOCTOR:	If I win, I don't want anything of any monetary value from you.
AHMET BEYAZ:	OK, so you don't want anything of any monetary value, but what do you want?
THE WINE DOCTOR:	To marry your daughter.
AHMET BEYAZ:	If you win, you want to marry my daughter! You can't be serious!
THE WINE DOCTOR:	Oh, I'm deadly serious, Mr Beyaz.
LEYLA BEYAZ:	But you can't bet for something like that! Look, is this a joke or something?
THE WINE DOCTOR:	Oh, it's no joke, Mrs Beyaz, I'm quite serious. I've really taken a shine to Songül, and I want to marry her.
AHMET BEYAZ:	Fine, but this isn't the way to go about it! You've

	got to talk to Songül, and if she wants to marry you too, then so be it.
LEYLA BEYAZ:	That's right, there's no need to bet for it!
THE WINE DOCTOR:	Songül told me yesterday on the phone that she doesn't want me. But I want to be a part of your family, and once we're married, I'm sure Songül will grow to love me.
SONGÜL:	Just a moment! Can I say something here? (*Turning to the Wine Doctor*) Now look, yesterday you tried to sweet talk me over the phone and pay me all sorts of compliments. And maybe that sort of thing works in France, but over here, no.
THE WINE DOCTOR:	What? You think you can do better than me, do you? But marriage is supposed to be made in heaven... Maybe you'll start to love me, you know, if we get married...
LEYLA BEYAZ:	Now you listen to me, you can't win a girl in a bet! Marriage is a serious step, and when you take that step, shouldn't you be serious as well?
THE WINE DOCTOR:	Oh, that's undoubtedly true, Mrs Beyaz, but don't you worry, I am serious, really serious.
AHMET BEYAZ:	It's impossible for you to win the bet, but even so, I can't accept this on behalf of my daughter.
THE WINE DOCTOR:	Why not? You're a businessman, aren't you? If you're so sure of yourself, you shouldn't miss this golden opportunity – after all, a good businessman is someone who knows how to capitalise on his

THE GOVERNESS

	opportunities!
AHMET BEYAZ:	Now you look here, I'm not one for getting something for nothing; I'm an industrialist; I produce goods, and I sell them. That's the only business I understand.
THE WINE DOCTOR:	Oh, you understand alright, Mr Beyaz, but you're afraid, afraid for your daughter...
LEYLA BEYAZ:	(*Turning to The Judge and The Judge's Wife*) What do you think about all this?
THE JUDGE:	Well, there's nothing wrong with having a bet for fun, but this, this is a huge gamble! It's immoral!
THE WINE DOCTOR:	But why? What exactly is immoral about it?
THE JUDGE'S WIFE:	May I explain?
THE WINE DOCTOR:	I don't see why not. I'm interested to see what you'll say.
THE JUDGE'S WIFE:	Well, as my husband just said, this is a huge gamble because you're going to lose a mansion worth trillions of dollars if Ahmet wins.
THE WINE DOCTOR:	But what if I win?
AHMET BEYAZ:	There's no way you can win!
THE WINE DOCTOR:	But what if I do?
THE JUDGE'S WIFE:	Look, the thought of a girl spending her wedding night with a man she doesn't want, well, it's revolting!

THE WINE DOCTOR: Am I revolting, then?

THE JUDGE'S WIFE: If Songül wanted to be with you, I would even say you were handsome, but if you force her to be together with you, then, to my mind, yes, you are revolting.

THE WINE DOCTOR: Well, if I win, I will force her, and I won't be revolting, not like the bilge coming out of your mouth.

THE JUDGE: Now look here, when you're speaking to my wife, you'll show a little more respect.

THE WINE DOCTOR: Sorry, I didn't realise I was being disrespectful.

THE JUDGE: Well, "bilge" is hardly a very nice word, is it? I would have expected better of you.

THE WINE DOCTOR: My friends, I do apologise, but let me explain. Songül isn't the sort of girl who you can meet every day. She told me she didn't want to share her life with me, so all I'm doing is looking for other ways to persuade her; it's as simple as that.

AHMET BEYAZ: (*Turning to the Governess*) Guvvie, haven't you got anything to say about all this? What do you think?

THE GOVERNESS: I never knew betting could be so amusing! I can't think what else to do apart from laugh.

SONGÜL: Hey, wouldn't you like to ask me what I think? I mean, I'm the one involved here!

AHMET BEYAZ: Oh, darling, I know you'd never agree to something like that.

SONGÜL: But, why not, dad? Maybe I would...

AHMET BEYAZ: What? Why?

SONGÜL: Look, you're saying that the wine doctor will definitely lose, aren't you?

AHMET BEYAZ: I'm one thousand five hundred percent sure of that!

SONGÜL: Well then, why shouldn't I get my own mansion? It's not bad, is it, to have something so valuable fall into your lap without having to lift a finger. But I'll only accept on one condition...

AHMET BEYAZ: And what might that be?

SONGÜL: If we do win, I want to live in the mansion by myself. You know how I keep going on about having a studio flat and how you never agree to it? Well, that mansion can be my studio flat! Oh, and I'm taking the governess with me.

AHMET BEYAZ: Well, darling, it's your decision; I know that the doctor is going to lose.

SONGÜL: Oh, but there's just one more thing I need to know, and for that I'm going to need the judge's help. How valid is a bet like this, legally?

THE JUDGE: Well, the sale or donation of real estate only becomes legally recognised once it has been lodged with the Land Registry...

SONGÜL: So, in our case?

THE JUDGE:	Well, it could be done by a deed of bargain and sale... So, if Mr Gün loses the bet, he agrees to sell the mansion at a price and at a time of his choosing.
THE WINE DOCTOR:	And what about Songül's situation?
THE JUDGE:	Well, if she loses the bet, there would have to be an agreement promising that she would marry Mr Gün. Because, as you know, a marriage only gains legal status in the presence of a registrar or other party designated by the registrar and with the signatures of two witnesses. And, of course, the bride and groom must state that they consent to be married.
SONGÜL:	Dad, could I speak with you for a moment in private?
AHMET BEYAZ:	Of course you can. (*Songül and Ahmet Beyaz go into a corner and whisper between themselves*)
SONGÜL:	OK, I accept.
LEYLA BEYAZ:	Are you out of your mind! Songül, will you stop being so reckless!
AHMET BEYAZ:	(*To Leyla Beyaz*) Leyla, please keep out of this!
LEYLA BEYAZ:	(*To The Judge and The Judge's Wife*) Don't just stand there! Say something!
AHMET BEYAZ:	Don't worry, me and Songül know exactly what we're doing. The doctor will lose. I'm not stupid, after all, am I?

THE GOVERNESS

LEYLA BEYAZ: (*To The Governess*) For God's sake, Guvvie, why don't you do something to stop this ridiculous bet!

THE GOVERNESS: Well, they seem pretty sure of their decision to me; there's nothing I can do.

SONGÜL: Just so there's no possibility of misunderstanding, let me repeat: Mr Gün will taste the wine that dad is about to give him and in the space of a few minutes, he will tell us where and when it was produced. If he guesses correctly, I shall marry him.

THE WINE DOCTOR: Within three days! A marriage of necessity!

SONGÜL: Yes, I accept. But, of course, if he gets it wrong, he will hand over the mansion he inherited within three days.

THE WINE DOCTOR: I accept!

LEYLA BEYAZ: I've never heard such nonsense in my life!

AHMET BEYAZ: Leyla, you're making me angry! I told you, keep out of it!

THE WINE DOCTOR: Well, it looks like we've come to an agreement. There's just one more thing though; could we put in writing? Something short... And our friends here can witness it.

THE JUDGE: Well, I certainly won't be signing anything like that!

THE JUDGE'S WIFE: Neither will I!

LEYLA BEYAZ: And, as Songül's mother, I'm completely against

	this ridiculous charade!
THE WINE DOCTOR:	So, none of you want to witness the agreement then? You're all afraid I'll win. Anyway, what about you, Mr Beyaz, will you sign together with your daughter?
AHMET BEYAZ:	Yes I will! (*Turning to the Governess*) Will you sign too, as a witness?
THE GOVERNESS:	Well, I don't think the Wine Doctor will win for one moment, but still, I'm not going to sign because this is wrong; it's immoral.
THE WINE DOCTOR:	But why is it immoral? It's as moral as any man and any woman getting married might be. Now, if I'd been forcing Songül into some kind of illegal union, then yes, you could have called that immoral, but our marriage will be completely legitimate.
AHMET BEYAZ:	OK, let's not waste anymore time, let's begin. (*Turning to Songül*) Songül, are you sure?
SONGÜL:	Yes, dad. But first, let's draw up that document, then I'm ready.

(*Ahmet Beyaz, The Wine Doctor and Songül go into a corner. The lights go down. There is a short piece of music, and the lights come back on*)

AHMET BEYAZ:	OK, friends, take your places at the table. (*Everyone stands side by side so that the audience can see them*) Now, Songül dear, (*pointing to the cupboard*) could you open the cupboard and take out the first bottle of wine, the one in front. And take

THE GOVERNESS

                      the labels that I've tied to the bottle. There should be three of them. OK, give one to the Judge, keep one of them yourself, and put the other one in this envelope and seal it. (*Songül does as she has been told*) And now, my friends, the wine label, with the year and the region, is in a sealed envelope. The doctor will take a sip of the wine and has three minutes to tell us its year and region. (*Turning to The Wine Doctor*) Is that OK?

THE WINE DOCTOR: Yes, I'll explain the rest briefly. If I cannot guess the year and region correctly, I shall give my mansion to Songül Beyaz. But if I do guess correctly, Songül and I shall be married within three days. Are we all agreed? Songül, do you have any questions? (*Turning to the other guests*) And do you have anything to say, my friends?

LEYLA BEYAZ: I can't believe this is happening!

THE JUDGE'S WIFE: Neither can I!

THE JUDGE: If I could have been sure it wouldn't upset you, we would have left by now, but I don't want you both to feel put out.

LEYLA BEYAZ: (*Turning to The Governess*) Say something, will you? We're not going to turn a blind eye to this farce, are we?

THE GOVERNESS: It's a nightmarish comedy, but let's see how it turns out.

LEYLA BEYAZ: Let's hope it stays as a comedy; I only hope it doesn't turn into a tragedy!

AHMET BEYAZ: (*Impatiently*) OK, OK... Songül, darling, could you pour a little of the wine out into the glass? Now give it to the doctor. Doctor, it's over to you...

THE WINE DOCTOR: (*Holding the glass that Songül has given him*) Friends, before starting this great test of my abilities, I would like to say a few words on the subject of wine.

What is wine? A drink. There are hundreds of different drinks. What makes wine different to all the others? Personality. Personality cannot be found in any other drink. Why not? Because wine is an unsolvable enigma. In fact, it would not be wrong to say that wine is a living being. To drink wine means to try to become one with this personality.

My friends, wine is composed of four hundred different elements. Let me be more precise. Thirty-four dozen different atoms, molecules and neutrons, smiling at each other, making friends and making love. Please, forgive my excitement, but, yes, they really do make love.

There are good-natured wines, and there are nagging, shrewish ones. There are honest ones and dishonest ones. Yes, wine truly is sui generis, unique!

Wine is mentioned in all world literatures. Here's an example from Omar Khayyam:

And lately, by the Tavern Door agape,

Came shining through the Dusk an Angel Shape,

Bearing a vessel on his Shoulder; and

He bid me taste of it; and 'twas – the Grape!

You see? It's not just a mortal drink!

Well, anyway, I'm ready now. (*Suddenly sensing that the Governess is about to leave*) Wait, Guvvie, why do you want to go all of a sudden? I know you don't like me, but you see, I'm going to marry Songül whether you want me to or not. So stay and watch the master at work one more time.

SONGÜL: Hey, when you're talking to my Governess, show a bit more respect, please.

THE GOVERNESS: Now, there's no need for you to fall out with the good doctor on my account, dear. He can say whatever he wants to me. (*Turning to the Wine Doctor*) Very well, then, I'll stay and witness your mind-boggling feats.

THE WINE DOCTOR: Thank you, but let me say that that kind of interruption wears me down – I'm having difficulty summoning up my skills.

THE GOVERNESS: Well, I shall be more careful in future.

THE WINE DOCTEUR: Thank you. And now, let me begin! Once I've taken a sip, I shall enter a transcendental meditative state. Just for a few minutes. Could you please refrain from making any noise whatsoever during this time? Even the buzzing of a fly could make the difference between success and failure.

And now, my friends, I am about to take a sip of this enchanted, this miraculous, this extraordinary, this magical drink! (*He sniffs the wine well, takes a sip, rolls it in his mouth as if he's gargling it before swallowing it with a gulp*)

God will make me become one with this stuff of legend.

(*Shutting his eyes tightly*) There's wind from all directions, the wind is blowing... A storm, a northwesterly wind, I'm cold, there's a whirlwind, there's a blizzard, I'm cold.

Stop, you squalls, stop! Let the sun come out and warm me up! I am a man of summer breezes!

The sun is rising in the distance, covered in cloud. Red clouds, green clouds, white clouds. They're smiling at me, smiling, so sincerely, so poetically...

My soul is enveloped in the blue. The rising and falling blue. The foaming, the frothing blue. I'm swimming towards my fate.

Where am I now? It looks like some sort of island... In the Far-East? No. In France? No. The wind is blowing differently here. The Middle-East? Why not? I taste the sincerity of a friend on my palate.

Yes, a friend. I'm swimming, swimming to embrace this friend, swimming, swimming, and this friend is coming towards me, I'm swimming, harder now... I'm somewhere full of beauty...

My heart is beating to the pulse of Istanbul.

Memory! Don't let me down! (*He pauses for a few seconds, sniffing the air*) I know where I am! An island... No, wait, four islands... Kınalı, Burgaz, Heybeli and (*he pauses a moment*) yes, yes, Prince's Island. I've reached the shore, I'm naked and I'm climbing with my weary feet. The stones in my path, the pine cones, the green leaves, the broken branches... Yes, yes! I'm at Aya Yorgi!

But which year am I in? I'm descending from eternity to life, coming down, towards the twentieth century... I've touched down. Happiness fills me and... I'm in 1950.

(*He opens his eyes as if he's coming round*)

Well, my friends, here's my answer: it's from Prince's Island and it's an Aya Yorgi 1950.

AHMET BEYAZ: Oh my God, he got it! That's right!

SONGÜL: But how, dad? How? How did he get it?

THE JUDGE: Yes, that is what it says on the label. You guessed correctly.

LEYLA BEYAZ: So what happens now?

THE WINE DOCTOR: Well, let's start the wedding preparations. Right now...

AHMET BEYAZ: But wait, you should give my daughter a bit of time... Why don't you both go out together for a while, win her heart...

THE WINE DOCTOR: A wedding within three days! Give me what I'm due!

SONGÜL: What are we arguing about? We lost. (*Turning to the Wine Doctor*) And you, like I told you twice yesterday, I don't love you and I don't want to marry you, but a promise is a promise... I will marry you, and the very next day, I'll be filing for

	divorce!
THE WINE DOCTOR:	But why, maybe you'll grow to love me?
SONGÜL:	Now let me explain something: I love someone else, and I'm going to marry him; we decided yesterday... Really, I swear it's true; I told the Governess about it earlier on today.
THE WINE DOCTOR:	But if that's the case, why did you accept the bet?
SONGÜL:	Dad was so convinced we'd win!
THE WINE DOCTOR:	Well, what if I'd lost then? You'd have lived together in the mansion, or what?
SONGÜL:	Actually, you won't believe me, but it hadn't even crossed my mind. We're wealthy enough as we are; we have no need of anything you could possibly give us.
AHMET BEYAZ:	Songül, darling, forgive me, and you too, my friend. Come, let's draw up an agreement. As you know, I've got two factories: a textile factory and an electrical goods factory. I'll transfer all the shares over to you right now for whichever one you want. One of them will be yours immediately.
THE WINE DOCTOR:	But, factories aren't important to me, Mr Beyaz! I want to marry Songül.
LEYLA BEYAZ:	You know, I really wanted her to marry you too, but you heard her: she's in love with someone else. And Ahmet is offering you a huge factory, just take it and we can forget about all this.

THE WINE DOCTOR:	No, I don't want it. Anyway, this discussion has gone on long enough! Don't go poisoning my moment of joy and pride, or else you'll be seeing another side of me...
AHMET BEYAZ:	What do you mean we'll be seeing another side of you? What are you going to do? Look, I'm giving you one of my factories; we make a fortune every year, and it's yours for the taking! And it'll save me from this misfortune I've brought upon my daughter, OK?
THE WINE DOCTOR:	I don't want it! I want Songül! OK?
AHMET BEYAZ:	What kind of a man are you? Have you no shame? Can't you see the girl doesn't want you?
THE WINE DOCTOR:	Now hang on a sec! You're going to be my father-in-law, so don't you go making me say something I might regret! I do have a sense of shame actually, but you, you're downright dishonest!
SONGÜL:	That's enough! Now, look here, Wine Doctor, I shall marry you. But don't you go around badmouthing my mum, my dad or the Governess. I love them more than life itself!
THE WINE DOCTOR:	I'm sorry, darling.
THE GOVERNESS:	Now look, I've had quite enough of this! I've had to bite my tongue long enough. It's time this farce ended. (*Looking at Ahmet Beyaz and Leyla Beyaz*) You both look as if you've aged ten years! But don't worry; Songül's not marrying this man.

	(*Looking at Songül, who bursts into tears*) Songül, darling, you're looking the worse for wear, too. Do you think I'd ever let you marry a man like this? Do you think I'd ever accept such a thing? Oh, my girl, don't cry, my little girl...
THE WINE DOCTOR:	(*To The Governess*) What do you mean you'd never let her? Get over it! I won, OK? God, you're worse than children, you spoilsports...
AHMET BEYAZ:	OK, my friend, congratulations, you won, but think about what you're doing: how can it be right for you to marry a girl who doesn't want you? I'm giving you a huge factory, now let's just forget about this bet.
THE WINE DOCTOR:	I want to get married! After dinner, I'm going to fax all the papers straight away to let them know!
AHMET BEYAZ:	Don't you dare! Look, I'm sure we can come to some sort of agreement!
THE WINE DOCTOR:	There's nothing you can offer me that would make me change my mind.
THE JUDGE:	Look, friend, you won, congratulations. But give these people their due, will you? Songül doesn't want you, and forcing her is, frankly, tasteless. Come to an agreement with Ahmet.
THE WINE DOCTOR:	Look! I don't want a factory! (*Turning to Leyla Beyaz*) Madam, you invited me to dinner, but I'm afraid I do not have time. I'm going to fax the newspapers to make sure the story gets into tomorrow's issue. I have to leave immediately.

THE GOVERNESS

SONGÜL: Let him go... You know I am going to marry you, like I said, a promise is a promise... But I have just one final request...

THE WINE DOCTOR: What is it? I'll do what I can to grant it, as long as it's possible, of course!

SONGÜL: I want The Governess to live with us until we get divorced.

THE WINE DOCTOR: But, darling, that's impossible! Anyway, it won't be necessary either: we already have a servant.

SONGÜL: (*Shouting*) My governess is not a servant! Got it?

THE GOVERNESS: Songül, dear, let him say what he wants. Anyway, what are you getting so worked up about? Aren't we all servants to our work? Why should being a servant be something bad?

AHMET BEYAZ: You've got a real cheek! But you can be sure of one thing, in this house, however much the Governess might be a servant, Leyla is too, and so is Songül, and me, I'm just their manservant!

SONGÜL: He's just trying to annoy you, with what little brain he has, of course...

THE WINE DOCTOR: Now, you listen to me! You'll show your future husband a bit more respect, or else...

AHMET BEYAZ: You'll not speak to my daughter like that! What happened to your respect!

THE WINE DOCTOR: You seem to have used up everyone's quota, Sir!

AHMET BEYAZ: Oh, so now I've been knighted, have I? Now, I'll tell you one last time, in front of my friend the Judge and his wife... They can be witnesses to this: take one of my factories and let's leave it at that.

THE WINE DOCTOR: Oh, no, there's no wriggling out of it! You should be ashamed of yourself! Call yourself a businessman! As far as I know, a businessman keeps his word!

AHMET BEYAZ: (*Raising his voice*) Now that's enough! I can never agree to my daughter marrying you, have you got that? Go wherever you want, tell them what you want: Ahmet Beyaz licked up your spit, Ahmet Beyaz isn't a man of his word, Ahmet Beyaz is a back-stabbing bastard...

THE GOVERNESS: Now that's quite enough! It's time to put an end to all of this!

THE WINE DOCTOR: Don't make me lose my temper! We had a bet, I won, and you're going to pay me what you owe, do you understand that? I'm talking to all of you!

THE GOVERNESS: The little voice inside me is saying go to your room, get your gun, and blow this wino's brains out.

THE JUDGE: Oh God, Guvvie, whatever you do, don't listen to that voice!

THE JUDGE'S WIFE: Please, Guvvie ...

THE GOVERNESS: Oh, don't worry, I wouldn't want to dirty my hands on this piece of... but I can't just stand back and watch you hand over your daughter to this disgusting little man. (*To the Wine Doctor*) Now, listen, I'm going to go to my room, and then I'm going to come back down. You, wait here! (*The Governess exits*)

THE WINE DOCTOR: She's mad! She's gone to get her gun. Your Honour, she's going to shoot me, do your duty! There's going to be a murder here!

THE JUDGE: I'm a retired judge, not a prosecutor. If you're scared of getting killed, find a prosecutor!

THE WINE DOCTOR: Stop that woman!

AHMET BEYAZ: Calm down, calm down! Oh, you're such a coward! The gun's not loaded. It's a keepsake from her grandfather. It hasn't seen a bullet in eighty years.

THE WINE DOCTOR: I'm not safe here! This governess, she's not a governess, she's an evil sorceress!

THE GOVERNESS: (*Enters holding a newspaper*) Oh, were you scared I'd come back with my gun and shoot you? Don't worry, that gun's got dignity, you can't use it on just anyone.

THE WINE DOCTOR: (*Nervously*) What's that newspaper you've got in your hand?

THE GOVERNESS: (*Nonchalantly*) I thought you might like to see what they've written about you.

THE WINE DOCTOR: You know what, you're really starting to grow on me. I'm touched, you kept the newspaper so you could show it to me!

THE GOVERNESS:	Yes, I thought you'd be interested to know what they've been writing about you...
THE WINE DOCTOR:	Well, they've been writing so much about me recently, bless 'em, and some newspapers just don't seem to be able to stop singing my praises; do you know, I find it embarrassing sometimes!
THE GOVERNESS:	(*Sarcastically*) I'm so happy for you.
THE WINE DOCTOR:	Thank you, and, you know what? For this touching gesture, I'll let you stay over at our house one night a week.
THE GOVERNESS:	Oh, I'm eternally grateful.
THE WINE DOCTOR:	Well, anyway, let's hear it then, what's this newspaper saying about me? I'm sure it's full of compliments, isn't it?
THE GOVERNESS:	No, it isn't; actually, it's quite the opposite.
THE WINE DOCTOR:	What do you mean, quite the opposite? What have they written?
THE GOVERNESS:	Oh, only that you're an illiterate half-wit, you know, that sort of thing.
THE WINE DOCTOR:	What? What do you mean, that sort of thing?
THE GOVERNESS:	Oh, well, let me read it out to you then. (*Reading*) "Orhan Gün, the man who calls himself 'the Wine Doctor', is a thoroughly dishonourable, cruel and despicable man who has difficulty reading and writing."

THE GOVERNESS

THE WINE DOCTOR: What bastard wrote that!

THE GOVERNESS: (*Calmly*) You can read it for yourself later, and that way you'll have proven to us that you do actually know how to read. But I haven't finished yet. Would you like me to continue?

THE WINE DOCTOR: Yes, do. Let's see what else that bastard has come up with.

THE GOVERNESS: (*Reading slowly*) "This so-called 'doctor' is nothing but a poor unfortunate swindler, con man, cheat, confidence trickster, fraud and charlatan." That's what it says...

THE WINE DOCTOR: The bastard! I'll show that so-called journalist! I'll tell his boss and get him sacked!

SONGÜL: Guvvie, could you pass me the paper a moment?

THE GOVERNESS: Here you go, dear. (*Pointing to the Wine Doctor*) Let him read it after you've finished, though.

SONGÜL: Oh, read it again, please!

THE GOVERNESS: Alright, dear (*she reads*) "This so-called 'doctor' is nothing but a poor unfortunate swindler, con man, cheat, confidence trickster, fraud and charlatan."

THE WINE DOCTOR: (*To the Governess*) Give me that worthless rag!

THE GOVERNESS: Can't you see I'm talking to Songül? Wait your turn...

THE WINE DOCTOR: Now, you listen to me! Give me that newspaper right now!

THE GOVERNESS: Why should I? It's my paper; I bought it...

THE WINE DOCTOR: What the hell? How much? I'll even pay a tip on top of it!

THE GOVERNESS: I'm sorry, but the newpaper is not for sale!

THE WINE DOCTOR: Look, Guvvie, just hand over the damned newspaper, or else I won't be responsible for what I do!

THE GOVERNESS: Ooh, what are you going to do? I'm dying to know!

THE WINE DOCTOR: Give me patience! Now, give me that paper and tell me how much it cost.

THE GOVERNESS: Well, I don't think you could name any price I'd be happy with. Is it really such a valuable article? How much should I ask for? I'm sure it must be as valuable as that mansion of yours!

THE WINE DOCTOR: Now, stop messing around and just give me the rag! Look, Guvvie, or whatever you are, I've got to send faxes and emails to the newspapers, I've got to let them know I'm marrying Songül, and I don't want to be late!

THE GOVERNESS: (*Sarcastically*) But you won't be sending any faxes or emails to any papers...

THE WINE DOCTOR: (*Sarcastically*) Oh really? And why might that be?

THE GOVERNESS: Well, read my lips, Songül doesn't want you, her father doesn't want you, the mother who bore her

	doesn't want you, the judge doesn't want you, his wife doesn't want you, and I don't want you. Now that's six people. And you're only one... Six to one, that's democracy.
THE WINE DOCTOR:	Look, I don't have to take this from you! I only have to listen to Miss Beyaz and her father.
THE GOVERNESS:	No, you don't have to listen to Songül or to Mr Beyaz; you have to listen to this newspaper article.
THE WINE DOCTOR:	(*Shouting*) You're driving me up the wall! Did I have a bet with the newspaper? Have you completely lost it?
THE GOVERNESS:	No, of course I haven't! Stop being so hysterical!
THE WINE DOCTOR:	(*Turning to Ahmet Beyaz*) Why don't you put your foot down and say something to her?
AHMET BEYAZ:	What am I supposed to do?
THE WINE DOCTOR:	What the hell have I got to do with the newspaper? Why doesn't someone tell her!
THE GOVERNESS:	But what's the newspaper saying about you? That's what's important here. (*Looking at the newspaper and reading carefully and slowly*) "A poor unfortunate swindler, con man, cheat, confidence trickster, fraud and charlatan, a liar and snake-oil merchant, a thoroughly dishonourable, cruel and despicable man."
AHMET BEYAZ:	Now, would anyone give their daughter away to someone like that?

THE WINE DOCTOR:	I'll ruin you all! I'll sue! If Songül doesn't marry me... (*Turning to The Judge and The Judge's Wife*) and I'll name you as witnesses, I do hope you won't perjure yourselves!
THE JUDGE:	Well, if that day ever comes, we'll know what to do.
THE JUDGE'S WIFE:	Your day will come!
THE WINE DOCTOR:	And there was me thinking such good things about you... But you've all let me down, all of you...
THE GOVERNESS:	Ah well, that is serious.
THE WINE DOCTOR:	(*Looking angrily at the Governess*) You just don't know when to stop, do you?
THE GOVERNESS:	Oh, don't worry your little head about that, you'll soon be leaving here never to return.
AHMET BEYAZ:	Let me repeat: yes, we lost the bet, but Songül doesn't want to marry you. I'm willing to give you a factory, fully operational and profitable, too... You just have to say yes, and everything'll be sorted and we can all sit down and enjoy the delicious dinner the Governess has prepared for us.
SONGÜL:	No, dad, I'm going to marry this man. You, mum and the Governess, brought me up to be honest. I lost the bet; I'm prepared to pay the price. And there's something else, dad. You worked night and day for forty years to set up those factories and develop them. You're not giving them to anyone; I could never accept that. They're the fruit of all

THE GOVERNESS

your hard work.

(*To the Wine Doctor*) A promise is a promise. I'm keeping my word. There's nothing left to argue about. But there's just one thing I want to know: why would a newspaper write such terrible things about you? What are you, really? (*Turning to the Governess*) Guvvie, could you read the article again, please, from beginning to end? Let's discuss what it has to say with our wineseller.

THE GOVERNESS: (*Reads or recites slowly and deliberately*) "Orhan Gün, the man who calls himself 'the Wine Doctor', is a thoroughly dishonourable, cruel and despicable man who has difficulty reading and writing. This so-called 'doctor' is nothing but a poor unfortunate swindler, con man, cheat, confidence trickster, fraud and charlatan, a scoundrel."

SONGÜL: But, Guvvie, when you were reading it our before, you didn't mention "scoundrel". I guess you must have skipped it.

THE WINE DOCTOR: (*Getting more and more angry from listening to them, shouting like a madman*) Enough! Enough! Give me the paper! I'll strangle that bastard with my bare hands! Give it here!

THE GOVERNESS: (*Calmly*) Here you are, read it yourself, that's if you can read.

THE WINE DOCTOR: (*Snatching the paper away from her*) Now, where are my reading glasses? (*He starts looking for his glasses in the inside pockets of his jacket; he finds his glasses case in one of them*) Ah, here they are.

	(*Opening the glasses case*) Oh, you see? I've left them at home! You see how absent-minded I am? I remembered the case but forgot the glasses!
THE GOVERNESS:	Oh dear, now where could you have left them?
THE WINE DOCTOR:	(*Absent-mindedly*) In the house.
THE GOVERNESS:	And which house might that be?
THE WINE DOCTOR:	(*Nervously, desperately trying to remember*) What do you mean, which house?
THE GOVERNESS:	I mean, did you leave them in that famous mansion of yours or did you live them in this house?
THE WINE DOCTOR:	(*Suddenly remembering something*) Oh God! Why am I so forgetful!
THE GOVERNESS:	Maybe you dropped them on the street on your way here... Let's go out and take a look, maybe some good citizen has found them and is looking for their owner.
THE WINE DOCTOR:	Damn it!
THE GOVERNESS:	Now listen... Today, you parked your car on the street, and you came into the house. Yes?
THE WINE DOCTOR:	Damn, damn, damn!
THE GOVERNESS:	You rang the bell, and the maid opened the door... Yes? Do you remember that?
THE WINE DOCTOR:	Damn it!

THE GOVERNESS

THE GOVERNESS: You said you wanted to visit the bathroom, and the maid showed you the way... Are you with me so far?

THE WINE DOCTOR: Where are my glasses?

THE GOVERNESS: After the maid showed you where the bathroom was, she went to the kitchen. She wasn't going to wait at the door, of course. You stayed in the bathroom for a few minutes, came out, and when you saw there was no one on the landing, you went into the room opposite the bathroom. Now, which room is that exactly?

THE WINE DOCTOR: Where on earth can I have left my glasses?

THE GOVERNESS: That room's Mr Beyaz' study. He keeps his vintage wines there. Now, who advised him to keep his bottles of wine there, who?

THE WINE DOCTOR: I'm sure I had them when I came here...

THE GOVERNESS: You did. Today is the third time you've been here. You knew the wine was kept there. Admit it!

THE WINE DOCTOR: Damn it!

THE GOVERNESS: Don't say that, it's blasphemy. Listen to the rest of what I've got to say: When you came here for the first time, you advised Mr Beyaz to keep the wine in that room because it was dark... Do you remember everything so far?

THE WINE DOCTOR: You witch, you!

THE GOVERNESS: You went into the room and headed straight for the shelf; you took your glasses out of their case, put them on and repeated what it said on the label of the bottle a few times to yourself: "Aya Yorgi 1950, Aya Yorgi 1950, Aya Yorgi 1950"!

THE WINE DOCTOR: Damn you!

THE GOVERNESS: I always though the French were supposed to be polite... Didn't they teach you that there? Now that room's got a folding screen in it. There's a couch behind the screen. When I'm very tired, I'll lie down on that couch to rest my eyes. I saw you when you came into the room, but you were so nervous and in such a hurry that you didn't even notice me.

THE WINE DOCTOR: God damn you!

THE GOVERNESS: Oh, I don't think He'll be doing that. While you were trying to memorise the name of the wine and the year, I knocked a thick book off the table next to me in my excitement. You were scared by the noise and immediately put the bottle back in its place, stuffed your glasses case in your pocket, but forgot your glasses next to the bottle. Well? Doctor?

THE WINE DOCTOR: (*Unable to decide what to do*) Look, friends, don't misunderstand me, it's all been a joke, I was going to explain everything. I just thought it would be more exciting if I waited.

THE GOVERNESS: You pulled off the same trick last month when you were here, but I decided not to say anything. Mr

THE GOVERNESS

	Beyaz likes having bets. And losing a tie in a bet is hardly important. I pretended I hadn't noticed anything that day for his sake. But today, well, today you really crossed the line.
AHMET BEYAZ:	(*Looking at the Wine Doctor*) So you knew all along! You utter bastard! Get out, get out! A joke? I'll give you a joke, you cheating little swine, you! Son of a...
SONGÜL:	Dad! What's his mother got to do with all of this? For all we know, she might have been an honest woman!
THE GOVERNESS:	(*To the Wine Doctor*) Come on, you ridiculous little man, come with me. We're going to Mr Beyaz' study so you can get your glasses and go. And don't ever darken our door again!
THE WINE DOCTOR:	You, treacherous... You're not a governess, you're a treacherous... hag!
THE GOVERNESS:	Come on, it's time for you to crawl back under your stone. (*Turning to The Judge*) Could you come with me, just to make sure he takes his glasses?
THE JUDGE:	Of course, Guvvie, with pleasure!
THE JUDGE'S WIFE:	Oh, can I come too?
LEYLA BEYAZ:	I'm coming too!
AHMET BEYAZ:	And I'll see this fraud to the door!
LEYLA BEYAZ:	Ahmet, you stay here, you shouldn't get overexcited,

	it's not good for you.
SONGÜL:	Can I come?
LEYLA BEYAZ:	No, dear, you stay with your father, and have his medicine ready, just in case.
SONGÜL:	OK, mum.

(*Exit all except Ahmet Beyaz and Songül*)

AHMET BEYAZ:	Oh, Songül! I'm so sorry; I almost ruined your life...
SONGÜL:	It's not your fault! None of us saw the man was a complete charlatan.
AHMET BEYAZ:	But the Governess took a dislike to him the moment she clapped eyes on him.

(*The guests return with The Judge in front, minus the Wine Doctor*)

THE JUDGE:	Well, he's gone, and I don't think we'll be seeing him back again!
SONGÜL:	Guvvie, if the same thing happened last month; he already knew the wine's region and year. Why did you let it happen this time?
THE GOVERNESS:	You're right, darling, I was going to explain, but the writer of this play came to the rehearsals, and said, Guvvie, I really enjoyed writing this play, so what do you say? Let's not give the ending away, let's leave the audience in peace to enjoy the play. And, well, we artists love our writers, don't we, so I

THE GOVERNESS

decided not to hurt his feelings.

Or the Governess could say this:

You're right, darling; it's just your father loves having little bets. Last month, he lost a tie, and what's a tie or a silk shirt to us! I didn't want to be a wet blanket; that's why I didn't say anything, but that cheat went too far this time.

AHMET BEYAZ: Guvvie, didn't someone mention Songül having a boyfriend and deciding to get married, or something like that?

THE GOVERNESS: Yes, that's right, let me break the good news... Songül told me about half an hour ago while you were in the garden. She's been going out with someone for three months, and because she wasn't sure until today, she didn't tell anyone about it...

SONGÜL: Dad, he's called Erol, and he's going to call you tomorrow to tell you he's going to bring his mother and father here because they want to get to know you.

AHMET BEYAZ: I like them already! They're most welcome! It will be an honour!

THE JUDGE'S WIFE: Congratulations, Songül! I'm sure we'd all really like to meet your future husband!

THE JUDGE: Congratulations, Songül. And, Guvvie, we should all be saying a big thank you to you, too.

THE JUDGE'S WIFE:	Yes, what would have happened if you hadn't noticed? Would Songül have ended up marrying that horrible little man?
THE GOVERNESS:	Well, it's all water under the bridge now; the nightmare's over. Come, let's eat!
THE JUDGE:	Guvvie, could I have a look at the newspaper, please? I'd like to see who wrote what about that charlatan. (*The Governess hands him the newspaper; The Judge scours it carefully*) But it doesn't say anything about him here?!
THE GOVERNESS:	(*Smiling*) But there is something about snakes and reptiles...
AHMET BEYAZ:	Ah, Guvvie, you're priceless, priceless I say!
THE JUDGE:	Well, I'll drink to that! Raise a glass, everyone, and let's drink to the Governess.

(*Songül fills the glasses. As everyone is raising their glass...*)

THE JUDGE'S WIFE:	Wait, wait! There's an empty glass on the table. The seventh glass, just a minute. (*She exits and comes back leading the Wine Doctor in by the hand*)

(*Songül fills the seventh glass, they all turn to the audience and say "Cheers!" together, raising their glasses*)

The curtain falls to the same music that was playing at the beginning of the play.